BOOK 4

FORTITUDE

Colonel Jonathan P. Brazee
USMC (Ret)

A Semper Fi Press Book

Copyright © 2019 Jonathan Brazee

ISBN-13: 978-1-945743-33-7
ISBN-10: 1-945743-33-6 (Semper Fi Press)

Printed in the United States of America

Acknowledgements:
I want to thank all those who took the time to offer advice as I wrote this book. A special shout-out goes to real Navy air warriors, CAPT Andrés "Drew" Brugal, USN, (Ret) and CAPT Timothy "Spike" Prendergast, USN (Ret.) for keeping helping me with "air-speak" and culture, and to my beta readers James Caplan, Kelly O'Donnell, and Micky Cocker for their valuable input.

Cover by Jude Beers

DEDICATION

Lieutenant Tom Norris, USN
Medal of Honor Recipient for the rescue of Lt. Col. Iceal
Hambleton and 1st Lt. Mark Clark from behind enemy lines.

Senior Engineer Valeri Bespalov
Mechanical Engineer Alexei Ananenko
Shift Supervisor Boris Baranov
The three men entered Chernobyl's Unit 4 to drain the water,
thereby averting a catastrophe and saving countless lives.

Both actions were the inspiration for some of the events in this
novel.

SG-88218

Chapter 1

Naval Space Pilot Second Class Floribeth Salinas O'Shea Dalisay felt for Dispenser 6's nipple in the dark and guided it to her mouth. She took a long swallow, the cold, fizzy Coke giving her an emotional jolt long before the caffeine could hit.

Thanks, Josh, she silently told her plane captain back on the *FS Victory*.

Carbonated drinks in the nutritional bank were verboten, but Josh took care of her, as always. She'd never had another plane captain in her three years as a Wasp pilot, and she counted her lucky stars for that.

The *Tala II's* cockpit was pitch black, and Beth hated it. Her imagination ran wild with what could be happening out there, and none of it was good. She looked out her canopy to her left, eyes straining to make out something, anything. Mercy Hamlin, her wingman, sister-in-law, and best friend, was supposed to be there . . . no, she *was* there, Beth assured herself, but she couldn't see a thing.

She turned to the right. Lieutenant (JG) Rafael "Scooter" Salamanca, should be right there, and on the other side of him, the newbie NSP3 D'andre Turbeville, so boot he didn't have a callsign yet. Beth couldn't make out anything in the darkness.

"Come on," she muttered to herself as she shifted in her seat. "Let's do something."

She was tempted to tell the *Tala's* AI to connect to Mercy on the S2S just to hear a human voice. That would be noted, though, and she'd pay the price later during the hotwash. Emissions blackout was emissions blackout, and Commander Vander Beek was much more a hardass than Commander Tuominen had been. "Creek" was a helluva pilot, far better than the squadron's previous commanding officer, but she ruffled more than a few feathers with her strict approach to leadership.

She couldn't even check her wristcomp for the time. It took almost no power at all for it to activate the implant behind her right eye, but "almost no power" was not the same as zero emissions. Beth was sure it was overkill, an abundance of caution, but orders were orders.

Sitting in the dark, she might as well be in a sensory deprivation chamber, and she'd long lost track of the time. It could have been an hour. It could have been a day. All she knew was that it had taken too long. Something must have gone wrong.

She was surprised when the small green LED flashed, almost too bright after so long in the dark.

"About time!" she said as she reached for the passive power switch and turned it on.

Her display lit up in a jangle of colors, and the cockpit backlight gave her enough to see what she was doing. She hadn't powered up her single FC engine yet. The energy bloom associated with that couldn't be kept hidden. Beth didn't care, though. Just having something to see calmed her anxiety, to be replaced with the excitement of coming action.

She stole a glance to her left. She could see a faint flicker of light from Mercy's *Louhi*. Their two canopies filtered out most of the cockpit display lights, but it felt good to know that she was right there beside her.

Beth ran down her checklist. When it came time to fire up her engine, everything had to be ready for a simultaneous light-off. She'd never done an actual one before. No one had, to the best of her knowledge. They'd worked the simulations aboard the *Victory*, but simulations were only as good as the AIs could make them, and AIs worked best when they could use actual data to create them.

She took another long swallow of Coke, this time sucking the dispenser dry.

Have I drunk that much already?

Dispenser 6 was the smallest of the four liquid dispensers, holding only two liters. That was a lot of Coke, and she had a small body—which meant a small bladder. Hooked up to her flightsuit's piss tube, she didn't know how much had flowed out of her.

The second green LED lit, and Beth ordered her engine to light. The *Tala* shuddered as the engine came online. Beth caught a lot of good-natured grief for anthropomorphizing first the *Tala's* AI, then the *Tala* herself, but Beth knew the fighter had a personality. She could feel her through her cockpit seat, more than a simple inanimate object. The *Tala* was ready for a fight.

The third LED flashed on, and suddenly, the stars were visible as the hull of their hide opened up. A purple diamond appeared on her display as Commander Vander Beek took over each ship in the flight.

"Kick some ass!" Mercy passed to her on the P2P as all 40 forty fighters took off as one.

This was the tricky part. No one cared about the hulk they were leaving. The "Q-ship," as the lieutenant had called it, was simply a lure, made to look like an ore carrier, but with forty Wasps in her hold rather than product. How much the exhaust of 40 Wasps damaged it was inconsequential. What mattered were the other Wasps. The exhaust from an FC engine, even at low power, could do a lot of damage to the other fighters.

On the *Victory*, fighters were launched on rails, the engines kicking in after 10,000 klicks. Their ambush hide had no rails, so the fighters were taking off under their own power. With only a few meters between each fighter, one leaving a split second early could scour the next Wasp, either knocking it out of the mission or degrading its capabilities.

The *Victory's* launch team had come up with a solution. Every launch would start at minimal impulse and was to be controlled by one single Wasp. Once out of the fake ore-hauler, the fighters would follow a slowly diverging course, the power for each increasing as the intervening space between them grew.

They couldn't take too long, either. Now that the ambush had been sprung, the enemy would react by either running or attacking. If the crystals ran, the Wasp flight could never get up to speed in time to engage them.

Beth hoped they would attack. She hadn't waited in the dark with only her thoughts for company for the last however-many hours to simply watch the FALs turn tail and run.

Beth was out of the loop as the commander's AI had control of each Wasp, so she tried to orient herself to the operational situation.

Twelve of them, she noted. *Four-hundred-and-nine kiloklicks away.*

Each Wasp had the latest and greatest shielding, the S-91A, but the "latest and greatest" that worked in the R&D labs often failed in the real world, and they'd just fired up their engines. Beth kept watching her display, expecting to see the 12 blips on her screen start to maneuver away. Even if this time their shielding was working, they had to have seen the sides of the bait ship open up. They had to know that this was a trap and that they were outnumbered, but the crystal fighters kept advancing toward them in two diamond formations.

I can't believe they fell for it, Beth thought as she watched the display.

Since the destruction of the megaship in the Battle of Retribution, as it was now being called, the "Fucking Aliens," FALs, had not appeared in human space in the same "hive" ship configuration made up of a thousand or more of their single-seat fighters, choosing to hit with those same fighters, but operating independently. Their targets were varied, but they were hitting more ore-carriers far out of proportion than anything else. Not just any ore-carriers—they hit titanium, iron, and lanthanum haulers more often than anything else.

Which was to be expected. The xenobiologists were finally getting a picture of what the FALs were. Humans already knew they were chlorine-breathers, but both their bodies and their spacecraft were made from the same basic metallic chloride crystals.

It was a weird concept—a fighter made of the same material as the pilot, as if humans flew organic fighters. Which is why Mercy had taken to calling their fighters "meat" ships.

And it could also explain why the crystals were pirating ore-haulers: they needed more raw materials to grow more ships. Yes, "grow." It wasn't proven as fact yet, but the general consensus was that they grew their ships out of solutions. They weren't manufactured as human ships were.

Beth found that interesting, but she was a fighter pilot, not a scientist. What was important to her was that these dozen FALs took the bait and were still heading their way.

"Reversion of control," the CO passed on the squadron net.

"Finally," Beth muttered, sliding her fingers in the controls. She could fly her Wasp through voice or manually, and she preferred the latter.

The crystal pilots kept advancing. Forty Wasps to a dozen FALs should be an easy fight, but the crystals had fooled the humans before. For every advance the Navy made to carry out the fight, the crystals made their own.

"Fox Flight, I need to you take the angel position," the CO passed on the net. "I want your scanners looking for anything out of the ordinary.

"Shit!" Mercy passed on the S2S. "How the hell do we get a kill if we're playing angel?"

Beth felt the same letdown. Her warrior blood had been rising, and to be pulled from the fight was like having the rug pulled out from under her. But it made sense. Thirty-six Wasps should be able to take a dozen crystals, if that was all there was. If this was an ambush on their part, then the sooner it was discovered, the better. And it made sense that the flight chosen was Fox, which along with Delta, had the newest software uploaded for their scanner console.

Beth flipped up her friendly overlay, and sure enough, Delta was heading "down" in a relative sense, the "demon" position.

At the limits of effective torpedo range, the twelve enemy ships finally seemed to notice them. They split into two flights of six.

"I guess the new 91-Alphas work as advertised," Mercy passed to Beth.

If the crystals had just picked the Wasps up, then Mercy was correct. There was no telling with them, though, and that was what made them so dangerous. To date, the Intel analysts had yet to discover any sort of tactical patterns in their actions.

Beth increased the gain on VQQ-48, but she couldn't pick up anything other than the wakes of the dozen crystal ships. Like a shark swimming in one of Earth's oceans, where its passage excited the phosphorescent plankton, so did any passing physical object disturb the dust, solar radiation, and micro-particles that existed in space. The 48 was designed to detect that passage.

"I'm not picking up anything else on the forty-eight," Beth passed on the flight net.

"I'm running the table, and I'm getting nothing, either," the lieutenant passed. "But keep on the alert."

Beth still didn't know what to make of her new flight leader. He'd graduated at the top of his flight school class, and the Stingers were no longer the uber-selective squadron they were now that the entire Wasp fleet was getting the upgrades and joining the fight. Still, that was pretty good indication that he was a good stick, to use the ancient term.

But he was *so* green and often seemed out of his depth. Between him and Turbeville, she didn't think they had 20 hours combined flight time—and she knew neither had yet faced combat. They were a far cry from Capgun and Gollum, both lost in combat.

Just a day before the mission, the lieutenant backed down in front of one of the ship's flight ops chiefs, which resulted in Fox flight having to sit around for an extra two hours before they could get their Wasps up-checked.

The chief hadn't necessarily been wrong—he probably was juggling a million things at once, but pilots like to know that their flight leader has got some balls and will look out for them.

Mercy was unimpressed with him, but Beth said he needed to be blooded before she'd make up her mind. They were all newbies at one time, after all.

Not going to happen on this mission, Beth told herself. *Not with us playing angel. Maybe the next time.*

Beth was a seasoned pilot, and she should have known better by now. It seemed as if the gods of war took a perverse pleasure in proving her wrong. As soon as she decided one way, the gods took it the other.

Not a minute later, the dozen crystals exploded into different routes, looking on her display like a slow-motion fireworks display. One second they were in a crystal version of a double diamond formation, the next, each was heading out on divergent courses.

The Wasps scrambled to meet them, the CO attaching each flight to a single FAL. That was ten flights to ten of the twelve crystals. And that included Fox flight. One of the crystals had broken almost straight "up," that is "above" their previous course. The CO's AI assigned that FAL to Fox.

Beth could hear the excitement in the lieutenant's voice as he said, "You heard the orders. Wendel, on me."

Beth wouldn't have chosen the Wendel. There were four of them and one crystal. The Wendel provided decent security against multiple targets, but it didn't maximize firepower forward, which could give an enemy a shot at taking out the lead craft—in this case, the lieutenant.

Still, it wasn't a horrible choice given the situation, so Beth stayed quiet and moved into position. If the crystal was intent on running, as it looked, and stayed on a steady course, then things should work out.

The crystal fired a salvo of four torpedoes. If it wanted to take out at least one of the Wasps, it would have sent all four on divergent courses at one of them. But with one torp to one Wasp, there wasn't much of a threat. It could buy the crystal some time as they dealt with the torps, but not enough to sway the outcome.

"Maintain course and engage torpedoes with your hadrons," the lieutenant passed, trying hard to sound calm, but not doing a great job at it.

Beth locked on and began to fire. At this range, it was hit and miss, with more in the miss column. The distance was closing, but in the minute or so that it took the beam to reach the torpedoes, the torps' defensive measures kicked in, juking one way or the other. Hitting one for any length of time was more luck than skill.

However, as the crystal torpedo sped along at close to .75 C, that distance was rapidly closing, which meant the time gap was closing, and the advantage shifted to the humans.

Beth wasn't worried. If her P-13 didn't burn through, she had her own torpedoes, but for this, she preferred her rail gun. For close in defense, it couldn't be beat . . . if a pilot had nerves of steel.

NP2 Floribeth Salinas O'Shea Dalisay had such nerves.

She left the P-13 targeting to the *Tala's* AI, then locked in her rail gun, programming it to fire as the torpedo reached five hundred kiloklicks, confident that the crystal torp would be destroyed. Then she returned her full attention to the FAL itself.

After firing its salvo, the crystal wasn't blithely running for the hills. It started pulling hard to its "up," which was to Fox' Flight's relative left . . . and that swung its route closer to crossing the *Tala's* path, flying in the number three position.

"Satan's Balls, Beth! You going to get another?" Mercy passed on the S2S. "As if you need another kill."

"Can't help it, sista," Beth said, her warrior spirit rising.

Beth had more kills than any other active Navy pilot, but she wasn't motivated by numbers. It was the thrill of the hunt, going one-on-one with the enemy, that motivated her. She'd been somewhat complacent, and observer, until the crystal changed the equation, and now she was getting eager.

The lieutenant had seen it, too, of course. He came on the flight net and passed, "Priority shifting to Fire Ant."

He sounded deflated, like a kid who was told there would be no Christmas this year.

Sorry about that, sir, but the vagrancies of war and all.

Beth was already well within torpedo range, but she wanted a sure kill. A little closer, a spread of three, and the crystal would be splashed. She was barely aware when Mercy knocked down the torpedo on her, then in quick succession, the other three torps were destroyed. She was focused on the beautiful ballet developing, two dancers intertwined in a death dance.

Twice, the *Tala* was hit by the crystals beam weapon. Twice, the *Tala* juked before her shielding was degraded by more than a few percentage points.

She cut the *Tala* in tighter a moment before the crystal flattened out its trajectory, obviously hoping that Beth would overshoot.

Nice try, but no.

She kept an eye on her targeting display, watching her probability of a kill rise by the second.

"That's good enough," she said aloud, ready to fire and ram a torp up the crystal's six.

"Take the shot, Fire Ant," the lieutenant said. "You've got it."

His tone froze her. He wanted the kill, obviously. Any pilot would. But there was just the slightest hint of self-doubt, of Imposter Syndrome. At least that's what she thought she heard, and all the years of having to prove herself to others and to herself came flooding back. She knew how it felt.

What had she told Mercy? That she'd wait to see how the flight leader developed after being blooded to make up her mind about him.

She knew what she had to do.

"That's a negative, Scooter. I've got a glitch in my firing release. You'll have to take the shot," she passed.

"Glitch? What kind of glitch?" he asked.

"No time for that. Come to zero-four-three, negative one-two-one. You'll be in position in less than two minutes."

"Roger that. Priority shifts to me," he passed on the net, his voice rising with excitement.

The lieutenant immediately corrected to the course Beth had given him. His firing window wouldn't be quite as good as Beth's was now, but still solid. And if he missed, Beth was still in position to pick up the pieces.

She hoped it wouldn't come to that. She'd seen pilots break after failing.

Beth watched the positions shift. After forty seconds, the crystal seemed to notice the change, and it started to react, but it was too late. The dice had been thrown, and all they were waiting on was to see what numbers popped up.

Slightly early, at least when compared to when Beth would have fired, the lieutenant fired off two of his torps.

Why two? There's only one of them and four of us. Use the entire spread.

Nothing to do about that now. Telling him to fire the third would undermine his authority, and it wasn't actually wrong.

The torpedoes streaked forward. At this range, the crystal detected them almost immediately and began evasive action, but to no avail. The first torpedo hit the target, or detonated close enough as to make no difference. The crystal ship vaporized.

Unvoiced screaming filled the flight net. It took ten seconds for words to emerge from the ear-splitting noise. "Holy shit! I splashed the sucker," the lieutenant yelled in unadulterated joy.

"Way to go, Scooter," Mercy passed, followed by Turbeville.

"Nice shooting. And thanks for covering my ass," Beth said.

"Oh, yeah. What was that about a glitch. Are you operational?" the lieutenant asked, trying hard to control himself and get back into command.

"It must have been temporary. I'm green now."

"Are you sure? We can't have a disabled fighter here in enemy space."

"I'm sure. I'll have Josh check her out as soon as we get back."

"OK, but if you have anything else, tell me right away," the lieutenant passed, still excited, but in control of himself.

"Roger that. I will," Beth passed.

Fox Flight started to come around to rejoin the squadron when the recall sounded. All ten targeted crystals had been splashed. Two were speeding away and out of reach.

"Satan's balls, Beth. Glitch my fucking ass," Mercy passed on the S2S as they headed to the system's gate for the return.

"Like I told you, he needed to be bloodied."

"And if he'd fucked it up?"

"If he'd messed up this easy of a kill, then we wouldn't want him for a flight leader, right? Better to find out now," Beth said.

"You're dancing with fire, Beth. If anyone finds out . . ."

"Which they won't. I'll tell Josh to find something innocuous."

"Which will piss him off to no end, Beth. You know how he feels about his *Tala*."

"He'll do it," Beth said.

"You gave up a kill," Mercy said with a note of grudging respect a long moment later. "Not too many would do that to train up a lieutenant."

It wasn't the sacrifice that Mercy assumed it was. Beth knew she could have had the kill. That was enough for her.

"Well, you know how it is with lieutenants. So cute now, but then they grow up, so, you've got to give them all the love you can while you have them."

FS VICTORY

Chapter 2

"Bug?" Mercy asked Beth as Turbeville left the table to refill his drink.

"Bug? Why Bug?"

Mercy rolled her eyes and said, "'Cause he's drinking bug juice. Look at him. That's his second glass."

"I think you're going to have to do better than that," Beth said, taking another bite of her chili mac.

Mercy was bound and determined to figure out a good callsign for the young pilot, and for her, a "good" callsign was one the holder wouldn't like. Beth was fine with that. Her first callsign had been "Ant," due to her diminutive stature. She'd only been upgraded to "Fire Ant" after her rescue of Bull during the squadron's first fight with the FALs.

"Bug" didn't resonate with her, though. Maybe it was because this was only Turbeville's second glass, and he had to drink something. Maybe it was because Mercy was one of the few people in the squadron to call the orange drink "bug juice," something she said went back centuries. It was a "Navy tradition," according to her.

Beth wasn't sure the old Earth navies drank the same beverages back then. Well, they did Coke, her favorite drink. She knew that went back to the 19th Century. Coffee went back even farther. But a simple, non-branded orange drink?

Next thing she'll be telling me that they ate chili mac back then.

She'd never had the dish before enlisting, but she'd taken a shine to it. Luckily, she'd learned to like it after already having her callsign. "Chili Mac" as a callsign didn't have the swagger that fighter pilots liked.

As if summoned by her thoughts of less-than-studly callsigns, NSP6 Justin "Fatboy" Grackle, from Bravo Flight, flopped in the seat beside Beth, saying, "Hey, nice run, huh?"

Beth didn't know the origins of Fatboy's callsign. At 180 cm and 80 kilos, he wasn't overweight. But he'd had it when he joined the Stingers, and a simple thing like a transfer wouldn't give him a reset.

"It was pretty sweet," Mercy said, beaming. "We splashed ten with no losses. I saw you got one. What's that give you? Four?"

"Yeah. Four. One more, and I join you and Beth here. Mamma's least favorite child makes ace."

Everyone was feeling good about the mission. It had been a resounding success with the most kills since the Battle of Retribution and without the staggering losses.

Beth's happy mood dipped, thinking about the losses during that battle. Commander Tuominen, Capgun, the rest. They'd destroyed the FAL mother ship, but at a heavy cost.

She shook her head, took another bite of chili mac, and tried to regain her good mood. Everyone should be happy. The crystals seemed to be withdrawing as if the Battle of Retribution had given them pause about invading human space. Maybe not withdrawing, per se, but they were not as aggressive as before. They were still hitting lone ships, either destroying or pirating them, but they were also losing ships to a resurgent Navy. Every week, more pilots were being fed into the pipeline, more Wasps and the new, upgraded Hornet unmanned fighters were coming off the assembly lines.

Humanity was on full war-footing for the first time in a century, and the first time in history united against a common foe.

"You'll get it next mission," Mercy told Fatboy. "That'll make four of us. You, me, Beth here, and Turtle."

By "four of us," Beth knew that Mercy was referring to the NSPs, the enlisted Naval Pilots. Enlisted pilots had only been authorized for the last seven years, and even now, not every officer was onboard with the concept. It might have been better in the beginning when the NSPs were primarily piloting shuttles and tugs, but now with enlisted Wasp pilots— especially with one of them (Beth) being the most decorated pilot on active duty—some of the officer pilots felt threatened. Add the unmanned Hornets, and that feeling became more pronounced.

But humanity was at war, and more pilots were needed and far quicker than could be produced in the officer and then pilot pipelines. Out of the Stinger's 50 pilots, fourteen were NSPs. In other squadrons, that percentage could reach 50%.

"How's the newbie?" Fatboy asked, nodding at Turbeville who was now returning to their table.

"He did OK," Beth said. "No screw-ups."

"He's so fucking young," Fatboy said. "Just a baby. You got a callsign for him yet?"

"I was thinking "Bug," Mercy said as Turbeville sat back down.

"What's bug?" the young man asked.

"Why 'Bug?'" Fatboy asked.

Mercy rolled her eyes again and pointed at his glass of orange drink.

"What? What's going on?" Turbeville asked, totally confused.

"I don't get it," Fatboy said.

"Satan's balls? Doesn't anyone know our traditions? Bug juice, Fatboy! Bug juice."

"What?" Turbeville asked again, his brows furrowed as he tried to make sense of what was going on.

"Red Devil here wants to call you 'Bug.'" Beth told him.

"'Bug?' As my callsign?" Turbeville asked, half standing in panic.

"Don't worry. I won't let her do that," Beth told him. "We'll figure out something good for you."

Mercy scowled but didn't say anything.

Turbeville gave her a wary look, then said to Beth, "Wow. I mean, 'bug?' Really? Thanks for having my six on this."

Beth used her fork to scrape up the last of her chili mac, then licked the fork clean.

Don't feel too confident, there, boot. I just think "Bug" is stupid, and we owe you a better effort. But you may like what I saddle you with even less.

Chapter 3

Three weeks and two missions later, both dry wells without a shot fired, Beth still hadn't come up with a callsign for Turbeville. Mercy had come up with a couple of dozen, each worse than the last. Beth was feeling the pressure. As enlisted pilots in his flight, it was up to them to name the young man. Delay much longer, and one of the officers would step in with a name, and once given, that was it. Like a bad tattoo, it was permanent. Just ask Fatboy.

Beth was one of the few to have her callsign changed, and that was only to add "Fire" to "Ant."

The problem was that nothing much had happened, and other than a curious propensity to raise the ante on a two-of-a-kind, Turbeville was keeping his head down. Quite a few callsigns were anointed for alcohol or liberty-incidents ("Puke" and "GUE" being two examples), but being stuck on the *Victory* curtailed much of that wealth of opportunities. There just wasn't anything to draw on.

There wasn't much of anything to do at all. The crystals seemed to be on vacation with attacks dwindling, and boredom was setting in. The pilots ran simulation after simulation, and Captain Rafnkelsson ran a daily ship-wide drill, but that was the problem. They were *drills*. There was no sense of urgency. The *Victory* was one of the pinnacles of human power projection, yet she and the rest of the task force were plying the emptiness of the black. To a sailor and Marine, everyone on board wanted action.

"Is it chow time, yet?" Mercy asked from the lower bunk, kicking the bottom of Beth's rack for emphasis.

"It's only been five minutes since you asked last time," Beth answered, raising her butt and slamming it back down . . . which did absolutely nothing to Mercy's feet.

Mercy kicked back up again, and Beth whipped her pillow around and threw it at her roommate, who blocked it, then slipped it under her head.

And now, I don't have a pillow. Smart move, there, Floribeth.

Not that she was going to ask for it back. She'd wait until after chow and grab it then. She started to check the time when her wristcomp buzzed. Blinking on her display, a message ran across ordering her to the ready-room.

"You getting this?" Beth asked, leaning over the side of her rack and hanging her head upside-down.

"Sure am," Mercy said, sitting up. "What do you think it is?"

It wasn't a drill, which would come over the personal and shipboard alarms. And it wasn't a mission brief, which would have been announced.

"Maybe we screwed up the last man-overboard," Beth said. "I told you to hurry."

"It's not like we have people going overboard on the *Vickie*. We're in a freaking space-going ship, for Pete's sake," Mercy said, standing and picking up her regulation pilot blues from where she'd dropped them on the deck and slipping them over her decidedly non-regulation "Who Loves Bob" pink panties.

"You know that's only slang for a headcount. If we get hit by some FAL torpedo, we're going to want to know where we're supposed to go."

"The FALs have run away. Now, are you going to get dressed?"

Beth slid out of the top rack, holding onto the rail until her outstretched feet hit the deck. At 4' 8", she could barely cover the spread. She opened the small locker at the far end of the stateroom and pulled out her blues, which she had hung up before climbing into her bunk.

She slipped the overalls over her regulation black bra and boxers, stepped into her shoes, and after a quick look into the mirror, stepped out of the stateroom. Technically in officers' country, the enlisted pilots occupied the last seven staterooms in the squadron area.

"You know what's up?" Fatboy asked as more pilots stepped out and started down the corridor to the squadron ready-room.

"No," Mercy said, "But they could have waited until after chow. I'm starving."

"They hold chow," Beth said. "Don't get your panties in a twist."

The pilots filed into the ready-room. Not just the pilots. All of the squadron's officers and senior enlisted, making it standing room only.

Lieutenant Salamanca caught her eye and mouthed, "Where's Turbeville?"

Beth raised her shoulders and held her hands out, palm up in an "I don't know."

"Turbeville, where are you?" she asked into her wristcomp.

"Sorry, I was in the gym. Just saw this," he hurriedly answered back.

"You'd better get your ass to the ready-room," she snapped.

"Five mikes. I'll be there."

Beth caught the lieutenant's eyes, mimed a bench press, then held up her hand, fingers splayed while she mouthed, "Five minutes."

You could have called him yourself.

And if he wanted one of them to find out, he should have asked Mercy. As the senior of the two of them, she was the assistant flight leader. In the short time he'd been with them, though, he seemed to defer much of the leadership to her. Beth knew that ensigns were taught at OCS to rely on their petty officers, but he really needed to take charge.

I've got a lot of work in front of me training him up, she told herself.

Turbeville made it to the ready-room, entering in a rush and breathing hard, ten seconds before the commander entered, followed by an ashen-faced Lieutenant Wysop.

"What's with him?" Mercy whispered to Beth.

Command Master Chief Orinoco called the room to attention as the CO made her way to the podium.

She took a moment to look out over the gathered leadership of the squadron before saying, "The task force commander decided this would be better told in person rather than passed on the 1MC.

"I hope you've all enjoyed our relative downtime, because that's about to change. The crystals have launched a surprise major offensive, seizing Ragnarök, Hell's End, Portland, and New Bristol."

There were gasps of shock at what she'd just said. Beth was as surprised as everyone else, and she just realized that the CO had privately told Lieutenant Wysop the shocking news before she entered the ready-room, and for good reason. He was from Portland, and his wife and three kids were on the planet.

"Time to buckle down, boys and girls," the CO continued, "because this shit is about to get real."

Chapter 4

For all the CO had told them a month ago that the "shit is about to get real," nothing much happened at their level. There was more urgency in the simulations, but real flight ops were curtailed while those on high tried to figure out what to do.

Agents were infiltrated onto the captured planets, and Navy scouts and drones snuck into the systems to gather data. The fighters stewed, waiting for their turn in the breech. And now, thirty-three days after the attack, it looked like that turn had finally come.

"How's Air taking it?" Beth asked Fatboy as they donned their flightsuits.

"Not good. I thought Doc Ellen was going to down-check him, but since we're not heading for Portland . . ."

"Air" was Lieutenant Wysop. He was one of 41 *Victory* sailors and two Marines with family on the six planets the crystals had seized: the originally reported four, Jin Tien, and Peace Junction.

"If the bastards had taken New Cebu, I'd want to be on the mission," Beth said.

"Yeah, me, too. I mean, if they'd taken Earth. But you've got to keep your head on straight," Fatboy said. "You can't go in half-cocked."

Beth just grunted. If her family was taken prisoner, nothing could keep her away. And if they'd been killed . . .

Don't think that way. Everyone's still alive on those planets.

"Everyone" might be a stretch, but from the initial reports, the death toll was comparatively light. The crystals had landed so quickly and with such force that the planetary defenses had been overcome in short order. Estimates were that the death rate could be as low as 5% and as high as 20%.

Still horrible, but when the crystals had attacked Farmington, the death count had been much higher.

Each of the six planets had mineral wealth, especially in titanium, iron, and lanthanum, the same three elements that the crystals seemed to seek out. Each had significant, but fairly low numbers of inhabitants. None of the six planets had much in the way of defenses, and there were no nearby naval bases. All of those were factors that the FALs obviously took into account to pick their targets.

Now, humanity was going to take them back.

Task Force Urgent Hammer, made up of the old Task Forces 39, 67, and 71, was ordered to free Ragnarök. TF 39 centered around the *Victory* and her escorts. Task Force 67 was a mirror of 39 with the *Avenger* as the flagship. TF 71 was a landing force of 62,000 Marines. All told, Urgent Hammer was a potent force, but Beth wished they were going in stronger.

The Navy couldn't afford to send out more ships, however. They had to protect the homeworld and vital planets from more attacks. Fully 75% of the fleet was in a defensive mode, leaving the rest to free the six captive planets.

"I wish we were Sixty-Seven," Mercy said as she fastened her throat latch. "Can't pile up the kills playing sheepdog for the grunts."

"Just be lucky we're in it at all. We could be back protecting Refuge," Beth said.

She understood her sister-in-law, however. Given the choice, she'd want to be taking on the FAL ship in the system, but that was left to the *Avenger* and her escorts. The *Victory's* mission was to make sure the Marines landed, then give them close air support. The last two weeks had been non-stop sims of ground support missions.

The Wasp was a helluva space fighter and a decent atmospheric craft, and the Marine Lightings were designed for ground-support. Still, 48 Wasps were nothing to sneeze at, and if they could help the Marines, all the better.

Still, Beth would rather be out in space taking on the crystal fighters. It was where she felt the most comfortable. She'd managed to survive an atmospheric dogfight on

Toowoomba when Mercy had been shot down, but it had been no sure thing. She'd take the cold reaches of the black any day of the week.

"All hands, man your transit stations," came over the 1MC. "Gate transit in twenty minutes."

"That's us," Beth said, standing up and taking her helmet out of its shelf. "Let's get going."

The ready-room opened directly into Bravo Hangar, and the Stinger Pilots made their way to their fighters. Beth had gone over the latest readouts with Josh two hours ago, but regulations were regulations, and she conducted a flight-check of the *Tala*. As expected, Josh had her in fighting trim. She signed off on the fighter and climbed into it, settling into the seat. Leaving the canopy retracted, she ran a final system check, then settled in for the wait.

Prior to the outbreak of war, fighter pilots didn't have "transit stations." Shooting a gate was no different than routine transit, something only of concern to the navigation crew. After the war had broken out, the procedure was changed with all hands given specific transit stations—not exactly their battle stations, but one level of alert below that.

For some, there wasn't much difference. The food techs stayed in the kitchens, the bridge crew on the bridge. For others, it was more of a difference in readiness. The Marines stayed in their berthing, but with their weapons and combat kits (which Beth thought was pointless. Who were they going to shoot their rifles at?). The Wasp pilots' transit station was in their fighters. None of the Wasps were powered up, but if the need arose, VF-51, the Exemplars, could launch within seven minutes, and Stingers could launch within another twelve.

Not that Beth expected to launch. Going through a gate was a chokepoint, and the *Victory* would be vulnerable, but the Navy knew this. Two scouts had shot the gate three hours before, and then the big battleship was preceded by five of her escorts. If the crystals were lying in wait on the other side of the gate, then the scouts first, then the destroyers, cruisers, and frigates would make contact long before the *Victory* shot the gate. This gate, just like the previous one, should be routine, with only the last one into the Ragnarök system possibly in contention.

"Hey, we gonna watch the next *Justice Navy?*" Mercy asked from her cockpit.

"We just saw Episode Six this morning," Beth said. "You promised."

"Yeah, yeah, yeah, but I need to know who Horti chooses before we shoot into Ragnarok. Who knows how long we'll be tied up there."

The two of them had promised to parcel out the remaining six episodes of their favorite space opera with one episode every two days. Mercy had a point, however. If they were running around-the-clock missions supporting the Marines, they could be tied up for a long time. And while not trying to be morbid, there was always the underlying knowledge that one or both of them might not survive the battle.

Beth was still willing to stick with their promise, but she wanted to find out just as much as her sister-in-law wanted to. She couldn't believe Horti was leaning to that asshole Rake, and she hoped that was just the editing trying to lead the viewers down the wrong path.

Beth gave Mercy a thumbs up. She wasn't the one to suggest breaking their promise, after all. Let the gods of broken promises lay it all on Mercy's head.

She pulled the nipple for Dispenser 6 and took a swallow . . . and got a mouthful of MD-3, the Navy certified source of all the required nutrients to keep pilots operating at peak efficiency. Evidently, Joshua hadn't filled the reservoir with Coke, which peeved her a bit. Sure, they weren't flying a mission of who knows how long, but she'd be sitting in the *Tala* for at least an hour.

Get a grip, Floribeth. He's taking a risk every time he sneaks the Coke in. Be grateful he does it at all.

She took another sip of the "mud." Mud 3 didn't taste horrible. It was just that it had very little taste, and what flavor there was tasted like liquid cardboard. Mud 3's worst sin was that it wasn't Coke.

"Gate transit in five minutes," came over the 1MC.

There were three "voices of the *Vickie*," one for each watch section. Keeping mostly to the squadron spaces, Beth didn't know many of the other sailors aboard the ship and none of the Marines, but she wondered about the three sailors whose voices were such a part of their daily routine. She and Mercy had a game where they tried to spot sailors who might be behind those voices. Mercy was shameless in walking up to likely strangers and asking a question, only to say, "Nope, not you," and walking away from her confused targets.

"Sunny" was on the 1MC at the moment. Mercy had originally named her "Sunshine Up Her Ass" due to her happy tone of voice, but that had proven too cumbersome, so they'd shortened it to "Sunny."

Beth leaned her head back in her seat, wondering if she had time for a quick nap. They had more sims scheduled over the next four hours after shooting the gate, and then she and Mercy were now going to watch *The Justice Navy* before they entered the Ragnarök system. One thing the military had taught her was to eat when she could, hit the head when she could, and sleep whenever the opportunity presented itself. She closed her eyes and settled deeper in the welcoming embrace of her seat. The Wasp cockpits were miracles of technology, but there was only so much in them. For most of the pilots, especially the larger ones, they were not particularly comfortable, especially for long periods of time. Poor Commander Tuominen was so tall that he had to fold up like a spider in a hole just to fit. For Beth, however, the seat was a comfortable fit, one of the few benefits of being on the smaller side.

Beth was in the half-awake, half-asleep phase, her thoughts bouncing around, when she heard Sunny say, "Gate transit in one minute." She opened her left eye, then closed it again, shifting slightly over to one shoulder.

She was barely aware of passing through the gate, that tiny wrinkle in the space-time fabric when her feet, stretched out in front of her, were lightyears from her butt. It took place so quickly that her body didn't know it had been ripped apart. Most people said they never felt the transition. Not so for Beth. It didn't hurt, but there was definitely something there.

"Transit complete," Sunny passed. "Stand by to revert to Threat Condition Delta."

"Hey, wake up, Beth!" Mercy shouted from the *Louhi*.

If she'd had more energy, Beth might have given her the finger. As it was, she just snuggled deeper into her seat. She'd have to get up soon enough.

"All hands, the *Victory* is now in Threat Condition Delta," Sunny passed. "Return to your regularly scheduled duties. Commander Hollingsworth, your presence is required on the bridge."

"Someone's ass is on the line," Mercy said as she started to climb out of the *Louhi*.

Beth opened her eyes, stretched, and sat up just as a jolt hit her which was followed by a dull boom that reverberated throughout the hangar. Immediately a the raucous breach alarm sounded, accompanied by a flashing red light.

Moving on instinct, Beth grabbed her helmet and slammed it on, dogging the seal shut.

"What's going on?" Mercy yelled out as she fumbled with her helmet.

"Damage Control Alpha, Bravo, and Charlie, report to Damage Control Central. All hands, remain in place until further instructions!" Sunny passed over the 1MC, her voice fraught with tension.

"Is everybody OK?" Lieutenant (JG) Salamanca passed over the flight net. "Give me a verbal."

"I'm up," Beth said, looking over and past Mercy's *Louhi* to where the lieutenant was standing up in the cockpit of his Wasp, giving him a thumbs up.

"Me, too," Mercy said, followed by a "Roger," from Turbeville.

"Are we under attack?" Mercy asked the flight leader.

"I don't know what's going on," the lieutenant said. "Just remain in place until we know more."

"If we were under attack, we'd be at our Battle Stations," Beth pointed out.

Mercy turned to glare at her, and Beth added, "Just saying."

The four Fox Flight pilots sat quietly in their Wasps for several minutes, the alarms still blaring through the hangar. Commander Vander Beek came on the net once to tell everyone to hold tight as she tried to find out what was happening.

Beth didn't want to wait for that, so she pulled up her display. Without a mission loaded, it showed the general situation, with the *Victory* just emerging through the gate and the escorts spread out. There was no sign of the enemy.

"It's got to be something mechanical," Mercy passed on the S2S. "I don't see any FALs."

"Neither do I," Beth said.

"So, do you think—"

Whatever Mercy was about to say was cut off with yelling as a group of red-clad sailors burst into the hangar. They streamed through the Wasps sitting on their pads.

"OK, these six fighters, get rid of them!" a senior chief shouted. "You, yellow shirts, that means now!"

It took a moment for Beth to realize the senior chief included the *Tala* in his count. She stood up in her cockpit to protest, but a blur sped down from the toolroom. Joshua had heard the senior chief as well, and he was rushing to protect his fighter.

"You can't just come in here and move the Wasps, Senior Chief!" he shouted, putting his slim frame before the much larger man.

"Get the hell out of my way, boy!" the senior chief said. "We've got to get access to the cyclotron, and they're right below this hangar deck."

"You can't just manhandle them!" Joshua shouted, not backing down.

"Better that than lose the *Vickie*," the senior chief said as he pushed past Joshua.

Lose the Vickie?

Beth stared at the Damage Control Team head in shock. The *Victory* was a hell of a big ship, and things looked fine in the hangar. Whatever was wrong couldn't be threatening the entire ship.

"You heard him, ma'am. You need to get out of that thing," a redshirt told her, only seeing her flight suit and not her enlisted pilot's wings nor NSP2 crow on her name patch.

Numb, Beth climbed down, jumping the last half-meter to the deck. The DC sailor looked up at the *Tala* for a moment as if wondering how to move her by himself when a team of yellowshirts rushed up, shoving him out of the way. The yellowshirts might not feel the same attachment to a specific Wasp as the pilot or plane captain did, but this was their turf, and they took pride in their ability to move the fighters around. Whatever was going on, they didn't want the redshirts to touch the Wasps.

Within moments, a team of four had the *Tala* hooked up to a bright yellow tilly, the Navy flight version of a cargo mule, and they were moving her off her pad and toward the rear of the hangar. The other five Wasps were being crowded along with it, leaving an empty spot on the hangar deck. To Beth's amazement, the deck was buckled, a couple of very visible wrinkles marring its once smooth surface. Whatever happened did it with a lot of force.

"What's going on, Senior Chief?" the CO asked after leaving her own Wasp and approaching the man.

"We took a hit. The cyclotron's been damaged, and we need to get access to it to shut it down. That's right here," he said as one of his team with a big vibro-saw and another sailor stepped up to the cleared space.

The second sailor held a device close to the deck as she studied the display. She swept it over several meters before she pointed at the sailor with the saw and guided him to the spot. That sailor dropped his goggles, lit off the saw, and applied the blade to the deck. Beth had to slam her helmet back over her head and step back as the blade bit in with a wailing screech, sparks shooting out.

"Why don't you just use the access," the CO shouted to be heard over the noise.

"Just were down there, ma'am. The blast buckled the frame. And we can't cut through that quickly enough. So, if you'll excuse me, ma'am, we need to get to it fast."

He took two steps forward, a clear dismissal.

Beth just stared, almost mesmerized by the stream of sparks. She wasn't sure what the blast was, but if it had damaged the cyclotron for the *Victory's* big hadron cannon, then it made sense that they had to shut it down. There were enough hydrogen ions rushing through it at near the speed of light to take out an enemy battleship . . . or cook everyone on the *Victory* if they broke through the coils.

The big problem, if she remembered the lecture from flight school correctly, was that when operating as designed, the particles were kept centered in the near-vacuum cyclotron by the same superconducting magnets that accelerated them. If anything disturbed that smooth pathway, the protons would collide with the sides of the cyclotron, the beam tube, she thought was the correct term, and that built up vast amounts of gamma radiation and heat. So, if the cyclotron was breached, the magnetic constraints broken, the particles would shoot out in all directions with a force equivalent to over 300 tons of TNT. Whatever wasn't blasted into bits would then be irradiated. Instantly, and with mortal finality.

Because of the inherent danger and heat buildup issues, the cannon's cyclotron was the most heavily armored part of the ship, even more so than the engines. This armored cell was located right under the hangar, where the hangar deck provided even more protection.

Beth stole a quick glance back at the *Tala*. She had a cyclotron for her cannon as well, but while her coil was a couple of klicks long and the beam eleven millimeters wide, the *Victory's* were multiple magnitudes bigger and more powerful, the coil several hundred klicks long for the particles to build up speed.

"What was that blast the senior chief was talking about?" Mercy passed over the S2S despite standing just a meter away from her.

As if answering for her, the 1MC kicked on, but it wasn't Sunny's voice that reached them.

"All hands, this is the captain speaking. I want to let you know what's going on. It looks like we were struck by a mine, which hit us at the QF plates. For those of you who aren't familiar with our system, the cyclotron cell is under the QF and QG plates.

"We don't know the extent of the damage, but the cyclotron itself won't respond to the shutdown commands, and the weapons cell itself is damaged to the point we don't have access. We've got three DC teams trying to cut their way in so we can do a manual shutdown.

"As a precautionary measure, I want all hands to remain in their transit stations. Department heads, pass out the emergency vac suits."

We might have to abandon ship?

"As soon as I get more information, I'll pass it to you. Until then, please remain calm. We'll get through this. The *Vickie* always does. Captain out."

"Holy shit," Mercy whispered into the S2S. "This is bad."

That's the understatement of the year.

A mine meant enemy action, which opened up a whole can of worms. Why did the mine activate against the *Victory* and not against any of the escorts? How did they know the task force would be coming through?

Mines were useful around planets, but in deep space? One of the assumptions was that the crystals did not know where the gates were, even if they knew how they worked. But if they'd mined this gate, then that blew that theory out of the water.

"Uh, Lieutenant? Our transit stations are in our fighters," Beth passed on the flight net. "But . . ." she trailed off, pointing to where their four birds and two from India Flight were jammed together.

"I . . . just . . . wait one," he said. He came back on twenty seconds later with, "Just stand here where we are, but out of the way. Stick close to the CO."

Meaning, if any of the ship' crew takes issue with us, we can point to the commander as our cover.

Beth took a step closer to Mercy, then watched the DC sailor with the saw attack the deck. He wasn't getting far. The hangar deck was heavily reinforced. It might be weak when compared to the armor around the cyclotron shell, but it was still much stronger than the rest of the ship. The captain said that three teams were trying to cut their way in, and she hoped the other two were making better progress.

Two more DC sailors appeared, guiding a piece of equipment that looked like nothing so much as a giant microscope. The sailor with the saw stepped back, and Beth could see he was exhausted, breathing heavily and sweat covering his brow. The big saw must be a beast to operate. The two new sailors trundled their piece of equipment up to the slight scar the saw had left in the deck, then powered it up.

"Goggles!" one of the operators shouted a few seconds before a beam of light splashed on the deck. Beth's helmet dimmed, plunging the rest of the hangar into darkness, but she could see the beam of light eat at the hangar deck, cutting a slick gash. Slowly but surely, the operators cut an opening, one meter by one meter. As the two ends of the gash connected, the chunk of hangar fell, but only ten or fifteen centimeters before it jammed.

The operator cut the beam, and Beth's helmet immediately adjusted back to normal.

"Senior Chief, it's buckled farther down," the main operator shouted.

"Can you cut it free?"

"Can't see much. Maybe."

"Hey, Scott, we can pull it out," one of the deck crew chiefs said.

The DC senior chief seemed to consider it for a moment, then nodded. "Give it a shot."

The deck crew swung into action, bringing up two of the same tillies they used to haul cargo or fighters across the hangar. Within moments, they had them on either side of the hole, cables attached to the strapdown connections. The chief cleared the area—a broken strap could cut a person in two—then gave the order. Both tillies strained to pull the chunk of deck out of the jam, and for a moment, Beth thought they'd failed. But with a sudden snap, whatever was holding the piece of deck gave way, and it came flying out, jerking the two tillies around with its momentum before crashing back to the deck right on the *Tala's* pad.

Beth swallowed hard. If they hadn't moved her, the *Tala* would be a piece of useless junk right now.

Beth joined the others as they crowded around the hole in the deck. She couldn't make out much, just a tangle of what looked like smashed junk. She didn't know what the space should look like, but she was pretty sure something more orderly.

A low whine emanated from the hole, but a whine that set Beth's nerves on edge. This was nothing like the soft, almost inaudible whine from the cyclotron on the *Tala*. Beth didn't need an engineering degree to know that the *Victory's* cyclotron was out of whack, and that was a dangerous set of circumstances.

The senior chief stepped back, hand to his throat while he subvocalized, and Beth edged a few steps closer, but she couldn't make out anything he was saying.

He intently listened to whoever was on the other end of his comms, then shouted, "Barrister, Skarg, you're up. See if you can make it into the cyclotron control."

Two sailors ran up, both with helmets, knee and elbow pads, and tool belts, reminding Beth of knights of old.

"OK, you know what to do, Barrister?"

"Yes, Senior Chief. We need to flip the green switch to shut off the power. If we can't do that, we need to cut the connector from the UB-52," the sailor said, patting a plier-like tool hanging from his belt.

"Alpha and Charlie still haven't made their way in yet, so it's up to you. And I don't think time's on our side, so get to it."

"Roger that," Barrister said, lowering himself into the hole, followed by Skarg. The two climbed through the twisted metal, disappearing from sight.

"Senior Chief, what's the status?" someone asked from behind them.

Beth turned to see the ship's CO, followed by a lieutenant in DC gear, the *Victory's* Command Master Chief, and three other officers.

"I've just sent in a team, sir," the senior chief said, pulling out his scan pad. Beth edged close enough to see it was a blueprint of this section of the ship. "They are going to take this conduit to QF-3-102-44 where there's an access hatch into the corridor right next to the entrance into the cyclotron control. The conduit's buckled . . ." he said before pausing, one hand held palm out to the CO for a moment as he listened to something coming in. "Sorry about that, sir. DC2 Barrister just reported that the conduit's pretty tight, but he's going to try to make it through."

"He's not going to try," the CO said. "He's going to make it. The cyclic variances are getting stronger, and the acceleration isn't going to hold forever."

"If it does crack, sir, the cell will contain the radiation," the senior chief said.

The CO hesitated, swung his gaze over those standing around as if wondering how much he should reveal, then said, "The cell's been breached. If the containment cell cracks, the *Vickie's* getting flashed, and that's the best case scenario. If the cell gives way, we've got ourselves a massive explosion."

Dead silence greeted his words until the senior chief asked, "Any idea of how long we've got?"

"It looks like about 30 minutes according to our sims," the DC lieutenant said.

"Then Barrister and Skarg better get a move on," the senior chief said before passing that on to the two sailors.

"Why doesn't the captain just shut off all the power from the ship?" Mercy asked.

"Remember what they said about our P-13s? They had to work out a way to convert and divert power from our MC engines, because on a ship, they've got their own stand-alone power sources that provide it in the right format," Beth told her. "But, I'd think that there has to be a cut-off from the bridge or engineering. I mean, fire control is in the CIC, so why not the power, too?"

"Seems stupid that they've got to send those two crawling around like rats just to turn off the fucking thing," Mercy said. "How about some simple redundancy?"

"I think the manual *is* the built-in redundancy," Beth said. "That's why they have someone manning the control twenty-four/seven."

"And where is this someone?"

Probably dead, Beth just realized.

The senior chief held his hand up to cover his ear, listened for a moment, then mumbled something back. He listened again, then looked up at the ship's CO and said, "Barrister's stuck. He can see the access hatch, and it's sprung open, but he can't get through the conduit. He's too big."

"What about the other sailor?"

"Skarg? He's bigger."

"Shit!" the captain said. "And we can't cut through it?"

The senior chief looked at the saw and laser, then shook his head. "No way they can get through."

"Captain? Twenty minutes," a commander said.

Beth could see the weight of command beat down on the man. He closed his eyes, took a deep breath, then said, "Abandon ship."

The commander whispered into his throat mic, and a moment later, Sunny's voice came over the 1MC, saying, "All hands, all hands. Abandon ship. I say again, Abandon ship. Move to your X-Ray stations. Boat leaders, debark when ready and take station two kiloklicks from the *Victory* until further word."

Beth's heart dropped to her belly. "Abandon ship?" She'd never thought she'd hear those words in her entire career.

"Get the commodore to the *Wapati*," the CO told the commander. "Tell Captain Addad she's got the squadron."

"And you, sir?"

"I'm seeing this through. Now go!"

Beth looked at Mercy, who was looking right back at her. Their abandon ship stations were their Wasps. That was how they were to get off the ship. But the six Wasps that had been moved were on the other side of the hole in the deck and the working party. They could not get to the rails. A Wasp could take off from anywhere on the deck, but under its own power, and the exhaust would fry anyone standing near them.

"Stand by, and let's see where this takes us," the lieutenant said. "We can launch in less than a minute if we have to."

"Command Master Chief Orinoco, you heard the orders. The pilots have their stations. Get everyone else to theirs," Commander Vander Beek passed on the squadron net.

Beth grabbed Joshua by the shoulder and said, "Get your ass going."

"But—"

"No buts. I can take care of the *Tala*. Get to Hangar A now!"

Her plane captain looked unsure of himself, switching from Beth to the *Tala* and back again.

"Now!" Beth said, giving him a shove.

He gave her one last look, then turned and ran to join the others heading to the Hangar A. Most of the ship's permanent crew were assigned to lifeboats and capsules, but the added compliment, to include the squadrons and Marines, were assigned to the ship's shuttles and gigs.

" . . . options?" the captain was speaking when Beth turned her attention back to him.

"I don't think Alpha or Charlie are going to get through in time. This is still our best shot. Maybe . . . Alexsova, are you up to giving it a try?"

One of the DC sailors stepped up. She was smaller than the other two who'd gone below, maybe five centimeters taller and 10 kg heavier than Beth. It was hard to tell with all the gear she was wearing.

She looked nervous, but she said, "Yeah. Let me try."

She started to step into the hole in the deck when the senior chief stopped her and said, "You're not going to be able to wear all of your protective gear. Dump it."

Already light-skinned, the blonde paled almost white, but she nodded and dumped all her gear until she was in her Navy overalls. She crossed herself and climbed into the hole.

"No protective gear? Won't that thing be leaking radiation if it's damaged?" Mercy whispered.

Beth waved her quiet.

"Does she know what to do?" the captain asked as soon as the sailor was out of sight.

"She's one of our best," the DC lieutenant said.

The captain ignored him, his eyes locked on the senior chief.

"She can handle it," the senior chief told him, but Beth didn't think he sounded that sure of himself.

"Satan's balls, this is all kinds of fucked up," Mercy muttered beside Beth.

The first of the Wasps from VF-51 took off down the rails as the yellowshirts rushed to get the next group in place.

Commander Vander Beek watched them take off, then said, "Lieutenant Salamanca, I've got to get to the *Stalwart*. Can you get the last six off?"

"Yes, ma'am. I've got it."

She looked like she was torn, but her Wasp had to move or else several more would be blocked in. Finally, she turned to the four from Fox and two from India and said, "Make sure you get out of here. If these guys are still here, tell them to get some cover, but don't stay onboard. There's nothing you can do."

Beth understood why the CO was leaving, and she didn't blame her, but still, she felt more than a little weird with everyone scrambling to take off while the six of them were standing around with their thumbs up their asses. It was really beginning to sink in that the mighty *Victory* could be about to die, taken out by a mine, of all things.

"Twenty minutes," the senior chief said, not bothering to sub-vocalize. "How're you doing, Alexsov?"

He listened to the response, then told Captain Rafnkelsson, "She's just getting up to the chokepoint."

"Senior Chief, should I get a ramlift?" one of the sailors asked. "It could help."

The senior chief looked around as if only now remembering that he had fifteen sailors still with him on the deck.

"Yeah, good idea, Sansuko. Grab one and get your ass back here. Go!" The sailor took off at a run, winding his way through the chaos of a deck launch.

The senior chief turned to one of the other sailors and said, "Lynne, take the rest and get them out of here."

The DC1 said, "But we're not—"

"Now, Lynne. You can't do anything here. I've got those three and Sansuko. Go."

He turned to look at the ship's CO, but the man was staring intently at the hole in the deck. The senior chief waved his hand at his number two, and the DC1 gathered the rest of his team and led them away.

"Now it's just us peons," Mercy said.

Not completely. As the senior chief said, he had four of his sailors, and there were the lieutenant, the ship's CO, a lieutenant commander, and the command master chief. No, Beth realized as she looked up. The ship's command master chief had left, probably to supervise the abandon ship. Everywhere else, sailors were rushing to get off the ship. Right here, fourteen were either watching or trying to save the ship.

"You holding up OK?" Beth asked Turbeville.

She was nervous, not being part of the fix, but she'd had a lot more experience than the newbie. Combat wasn't the same thing as this, but at least she'd faced danger before.

"Yeah, I'm OK. Welcome to the fleet," he said, his voice catching.

She gave his arm a pat and said, "You heard the CO. We'll be out of here before that thing cracks open."

He shrugged his shoulders as if it was no big deal, but she could see that it was.

More of the fighters took off, and with VF-51 gone, it was time to start with the Stingers. The yellowshirts were maneuvering the first of them to the launch rails.

"Sucks to be them," Beth told Mercy. "They've got to wait until the last are launched before they can abandon ship."

"You mean it sucks to be us. We can't leave until they do," she said.

"We've still got plenty of time."

Despite reassuring her sister-in-law, Beth couldn't help but check. If the DC lieutenant was right, they had about fifteen minutes.

"Mother fuck!" the senior chief shouted, before turning to the CO and saying, "Sorry for that, sir, but they're coming back out."

"Who's coming out?"

"All three of them. Alexsov's hurt. I don't know how she did it or how bad it is."

The CO stepped into the hole and bent over to try and see down the conduit. A moment later, he was pulling a bloody Alexov out of the hole, handing her to the senior chief and the lieutenant. She was holding her side, blood welling up between her fingers, her overalls torn and filthy.

"I'm sorry! I thought I could push my way through," she gasped between sobs. "I was almost there!"

The lieutenant laid her on the deck while the next two sailors climbed out. They looked almost as bad as Alexsov, just minus the huge gash.

The senior chief grabbed Barrister, who said, "She kept pushing, saying she almost had it while the fucking wreckage cut her. I had to pull her back."

"Is it bad?"

"I could see her guts, Senior Chief. Yeah, she's bad."

Sansuko came running back with a jack of some sort. He saw Alexsov, dropped the jack with a thump, and rushed to her side.

"What happened to Kara?"

"Sansuko, you and Skarg, take Alexsov to the sickbay shuttle. Not our escape pods. Leave the *Vickie* with the sick, if the docs let you. If not, you've got to get to your assigned pods. Got it?"

"Will they have time?" the DC lieutenant asked the senior chief as they watched the two carry their companion across the now almost empty hangar.

"I hope to God they do," the senior chief said.

"When are we going?" Jelly, one of the India Flight pilots, asked Lieutenant (JG) Salamanca, his eyes locked on the bleeding Alexsov. "We need to go."

The second to last set of fighters was taking off, and the yellowshirts were almost flying to get the last ones up to the rails. Their urgency was palpable.

"Not until they leave and these here clear out," the lieutenant   said. We've still got time."

"Well, tell them to get out of the way. I'm not sticking around here until the damned cyclotron cracks wide open," Jelly said, his voice rising an octave.

"You'll go when I tell you," the lieutenant snapped, putting some command in his voice.

Beth nodded in appreciation. Her JG was growing a pair, and she approved. He was almost as much as a newbie as Turbeville, but he was beginning to fit into the role.

She turned back to the CO, who was still standing up to his chest in the hole.

"What now? What're our options?"

"I . . . I don't know, sir. I . . ." he said trailing off.

"I think it's time, sir," his lieutenant commander said. "We need to go."

"How many are off?" he asked.

"We're at fifty-two percent right now, sir."

"Come on, let's mount up," Lieutenant (JG) Salamanca said. "We need to be ready to move."

Five pilots turned to get to their fighters, but Beth stayed where she was, listening to the two officers.

"And what will we have off when . . .?"

"Maybe eighty, ninety percent, sir."

Beth felt a wave of nausea wash over her. Eighty percent meant twenty percent, about six hundred sailors and Marines who wouldn't make it off in time. Her vision narrowed, and she felt faint.

"I should have ordered it sooner!" the captain almost wailed.

"You didn't know the extent of the damage, sir. And twelve-point-nine-point three specifically states—"

"I don't give a good goddamn what the regulations state! This is my ship, and I am the sole authority on it. I should have given the order earlier."

Beth started walking up to them without even realizing it. She didn't make a conscious decision about anything. Her body was moving almost without her volition.

"Dalisay, get in your Wasp!" the lieutenant yelled out, followed almost immediately by a louder "Beth!" from Mercy.

Beth ignored them.

She stood at the edge of the hole for only a moment, facing the CO's back, before she started shucking her flight suit.

"What are you doing?" the senior chief asked, causing the CO to turn around, his head at Beth's knee level.

"I'm smaller than Alexsov. Maybe I can make it," she said, surprised at how calm her voice sounded.

"But you don't know what you're doing. You're a zoomie, not a real sailor," he said.

"Maybe you can," the CO said, scrambling out of the hole and helping Beth with her flightsuit.

"Beth, what the hell are you doing?" Mercy passed on the S2S.

"Tell *Ina* and Rocky that I love them. I love you, too."

"I won't have to tell them anything if you just get your ass—"

Beth cut the connection.

"Tell me what to do," she told the senior chief.

He stared at her for a long moment until the CO said, "Tell her."

"Can she fit through?" he asked Barrister, who was sitting on the deck, breathing heavily.

"Maybe. It'll be close," he managed to get out between breaths. "With the ramlift, if it can move the wreckage a few centimeters, she probably can."

The senior chief grabbed the ramlift and started to get into the hole when Barrister said, "Uh, no insult intended, Senior Chief, but you've got quite a chief's gut going there."

"So, what the fuck are you getting at?" the senior chief asked.

"You aren't going to be able to make it to the choke point. It was hard enough for me."

"Just tell me how to use it," Beth said, reaching for the ramlift and almost dropping it. She hadn't realized how heavy it was.

"Look, she's not going to be able to push that thing in front of her. She's as weak as a kitten," the senior chief said.

"How about me?" the CO, the DC lieutenant, and the lieutenant commander asked in unison.

"Maybe you, sir," Barrister said to the lieutenant commander. "But, I'll do it. I know I can make it."

The sailor started to stand, stumbled, and went back down to his hands and knees. He was spent.

"I'll do it," Turbeville said, coming over from his Wasp. "I know how to use that bad boy."

Turbeville was taller than Barrister, but he had about the same frame.

"Then go!" the CO shouted. "We've got no time to waste."

"I need to tell her what to do," the senior chief said.

"Tell her on the way."

"Oh, hell. Here, take this," he said, handing her a pair of pliers of some sort. "I'll brief you. Turn to the DC 1 freq."

Turbeville jumped into the hole and started worming his way into the conduit. Beth inserted her earbuds, which should work anywhere within a couple hundred meters from her helmet, then gave the command to change the freq.

"Am I on?" she asked.

"Got you. Now go!"

The CO helped her into the hole, then said, "Go with God," as she brought her cross to her lips for a kiss, stuffed it back inside her longjohns, then ducked into the rent. She fell more than climbed down into the conduit. Turbeville's feet were ahead of her, and she focused on them. Without her flight suit, her long johns gave her almost no protection, and her knees were getting banged up as she scrambled after the junior pilot, but she barely noticed. All she could think of was the time ticking away as the senior chief droned on.

The crux was simple. Turn the manual switch, and if that didn't work, cut the power lead to the control console. He kept repeating it.

She ran into Turbeville's feet, bruising her lip.

"What're you doing?" she snapped.

"It's a little tight here."

"Just get through it. We don't have time."

He moved forward, then twisted around, and scooted through on his butt. Beth had it easier. The warped metal was jagged, and she scraped her arms, but she fit through with centimeters to spare. The next ten meters were relatively easy going, and they both scooted ahead.

And then came the real chokepoint. The side and overhead had collapsed as if a giant had smashed the conduit with a huge fist. The remaining clear space looked small, and Beth wondered if she'd made a big mistake. The opening was tiny, then a little farther in, a single shard reached up. It was covered in blood, and more blood still dripped out of her sight.

She couldn't imagine Alexsov trying to push her body through that knife-like blade.

"Get that thing ready. If I need it, I'll tell you. But don't do anything until then. We don't know how stable this is," she told Turbeville before passing to the senior chief, "I'm at the choke point. I can see the access hatch on the other side."

Here goes nothing, she told herself as she wormed her way, headfirst, into the opening.

Beth wasn't given to claustrophobia. She'd been tested for that before she ever became a commercial scout pilot. But she'd never expected to be worming through a damaged ship that was about to be blasted and bathed in lethal radiation while it creaked and groaned around her.

"What's your situation, Dalisay?" the senior chief kept asking her.

Beth tuned him out. She grabbed the shard, hoping to pull herself forward, then whipped her hand back as blood poured from the cut in her palm. She inch-wormed up, then decided to try and slide past the left side of the hunk of metal. She got her face past, then her shoulders, just sliding her breasts past, the edge scoring her longjohns.

Now comes the tricky part.

The deck bent upwards, and that meant Beth had to as well . . . and that drove the hunk of metal into her gut. This is what did in Alexsov. She marveled at the woman's perseverance, but Beth couldn't afford to do the same. She had to get through.

"D'Andre! I need a little more room. Try the jack thing."

"OK. I'm going to go slow."

"No time! Get it done."

"If I go too quickly, it can shift," he said.

Shift and squish me.

But she had to get through. She was committed, for good or bad.

"Just do it."

She was breathing as shallowly as she could, extremely conscious of the metal pressing against her belly. Each breath caused it to press deeper into her.

There was a hum behind her, and the metal conduit began to groan. Miraculously, the overhead part started to rise ever-slow-slightly, and Beth started to squirm forward when it slipped and crashed down again.

"Are you OK?" a worried Turbeville shouted out.

She took a quick inventory. She'd managed to move forward a few centimeters, just enough that the metal blade was now pressed between her legs. Her left thigh, right below her crotch, was cut, she knew, but she couldn't feel anything pulsing out of her.

"I'm good. About pissed my longjohns, though."

"Oh, fuck. I was so scared."

"I'm still stuck, though. Give me another lift."

"Give me strength," Turbeville muttered, then the whine of the ram filled the space again.

The moment she had space again, she scrambled through.

"I'm through! Stop that ram and get the hell out of here now!" she yelled back at the younger pilot before reporting to the senior chief.

"You've got five minutes," the senior chief told her as she reached the access hatch, then squirmed over the side, hanging on the edge before dropping to the deck below.

She was bleeding from her hand and inner thigh, the leg of her longjohns cut and hanging off, but all of her parts worked. The bulkhead to the cyclotron was gashed open. She took a quick look inside the rent, spotting the gleaming outer tube of the cyclotron. She could almost sense the protons racing around inside of it, 11,000 circuits per second, and that made her nerves crawl. She didn't need the cyclotron itself, however. She wanted the control console.

"Have the last of the Wasps taken off?" she asked the senior chief as she turned and jogged to the aft of the ship.

"Yeah, they just took off. The one pilot, the one with the half-shaved head, said you'd better live through this or she's going to kick your ass in hell."

"That's my Mercy," Beth said with a laugh, which lifted a weight off her shoulders. The weight fell back hard when she ran into the end of the corridor.

The corridor wasn't designed to end there. Something had crushed this section of the ship, and there was no going forward. She looked up at the frame numbers. The console was just ahead, but it might as well be a klick. There was no way she could cut through that with just a pair of Navy pliers the senior chief had given her.

"Senior Chief, the corridor just ended. I can't go any farther."

"What do you mean? It can't just end."

"I mean, it's crushed, like an old toothpaste tube. I can't get to the hatch into the control room."

"Where are you? What frame?" he asked.

"QF-three, one-oh-two, forty," she said.

"Fucking forty? That's just four meters away. You can't force your way in?"

"No. Sorry, but no way."

"We're down to four minutes. You've got to find a way in. You don't see anything?" the senior chief asked, his voice rising in panic.

"Not here. Back, the bulkhead buckled and split. I could see the cyclotron."

"No, you didn't. If you could see anything, it was the containment shell, not the . . . fuck, what am I thinking? Can you get through that? Like inside?" he said, hope creeping into his voice.

"I don't know. I didn't try."

"Well, try, god damn it! Run!"

Beth sprinted back down the corridor. The rent started only ten meters behind her, but it was way too small for her to slide through. It gradually widened, and after another 20 meters, just before she reached a major frame strut, the rent warped, giving her just the opening she needed. She jumped up headfirst through the hole, then struggled to pull herself through. The blood on her hands and thigh might have acted as a lubricant, and she fell onto a grated platform that ran alongside the cyclotron shell. Low lights ran along the platform, letting her see.

"I'm in!" she shouted in excitement.

"Now run aft to the control room."

Beth got to her feet and ran back along the platform, the cyclotron a menacing mass beside her, the uneven whine rising in pitch. She could almost feel the radiation reach out for her as she spotted the hatch and yanked, that is tried to yank it open. It refused to budge.

"No! You can't do this to me!"

She put up her right foot, placed is beside the handle, and heaved, straining her body until she thought her gut would pop. She thought it moved ever so slightly, so she gathered herself, took a deep breath, and yanked . . . and the hatch flung open, throwing her to the deck.

She darted inside and slipped on something dark red and wet. An alarm was going off, a calm, reasoned AI-generated voice saying, "Radiation alert. Implement Condition Alpha. Radiation alert. Implement Condition Alpha."

"I'm inside. The control panel is . . . it's gone," she whispered.

The control console was supposed to be on the far side of the control room, next to the hatch. Whatever had crushed the passage outside had also demolished the panel, which would explain why the bridge couldn't shut the thing down. It ran through the panel. Stupid engineering, but it was what it was.

"It can't be gone," the senior chief said.

"It's here, but it's crushed. I can't see the switch."

"What about the generator?"

Beth turned to the generator, or at least, part of it. Most of the fusion plant's working parts were shielded and under the deck. It was silent, but the green flashing indicator light was evidence that it was pouring power to the cyclotron.

"It's here," Beth said, before jumping as a screech emanated from the cyclotron. "How much time do I have?"

"We're on borrowed time now, so don't worry about it. Now, take out those cutters I gave you. Do you have them?"

Beth had thought they were pliers, but as she looked, she could see a cutting edge and what looked like a ratcheting mechanism.

"I've got them."

"OK. Now listen. Do you see the big cable that goes through the bulkhead?"

"Yeah, I see it," Beth said, kneeling and opening the cutters, placing the cutting jaws around the cables.

"Don't touch that," the senior chief said just as she started to compress the handles. "That'll fry you where you stand. Follow that cable back up to where it enters the reactor housing."

Now you tell me she thought as she froze, then gently released the pressure on the handles.

She wiped her brow and followed the cable up to where it disappeared into the housing, next to a cover that said "Do Not Open." A crash of something breaking reached her, and she forced that from her mind.

"Open the access cover."

Beth reached up with her right hand, and it slipped on something wet. Not just wet. Chunky. She refused to acknowledge that there had been at least one fellow sailor in the room, and they'd probably been over at the console when the explosion smashed it.

She shoved the chunky bit away, then cut the simple lock holding the cover in place.

"A radiation alarm's going off," she said.

"Don't worry about it. If you're still alive, the shell is mostly intact, and that's just stray radiation. But it won't be for long, so, have you opened the cover?"

"Yes, I've got it open," she said, wondering what constituted "stray radiation." As far as she was concerned, any radiation was a bad thing.

"Look inside and tell me what you see."

"I can't see anything."

"What? According to this, you should—"

"I'm not tall enough to look inside," Beth interrupted, her nerves approaching the breaking point.

"For fuck's sake. Get something to stand on!"

Beth looked around. If there were seats in the room, they were on the other side in the wreckage. There was nothing. With a sigh, and ignoring the bloody mess that had splattered the top of the generator, she grabbed the cover and hauled herself up. With one hand holding her up, she looked into the access point.

"I can see inside. There are a bunch of lights, some displays with numbers, uh . . ."

"Do you see a black lever, about five centimeters long? If not, you're going to have to remove the—"

"Yeah, I see it."

"Thank God for that. Flip it to the left until it is pointing straight down."

That's it? That's all I have to do?

After all she'd gone through, that seemed anti-climatic, but she wasn't going to argue with that.

It was hard for Beth to stay in place, but by scrambling with her legs and hanging on with her right arm, she managed to flip the lever the 90 degrees.

"Warning. Shutting down the generator will result in a permanent loss of power. The generator cannot be restarted," came out from the panel, startling her, and Beth fell back to the deck.

From outside the control room, the piercing sounds of tortured metal drowned out both the warning and the senior chief's voice in her earbud. Beth knew she had to act, but she couldn't hear the senior chief.

She stood and jumped back up on the generator, pulling herself with her right hand and reaching in with her gashed left hand to turn the switch another 90-degrees to the left.

"Generator shut down. Begin hibernation procedures," Beth could barely make out over the noise.

The green indicator light on the top of the generator turned red, but the horrible racket from outside the control room continued.

"No! I just shut it down!" Beth shouted in defiance.

She ran out the hatch and started pounding on the shell of the cyclotron, screaming in frustration, leaving bloody hand marks on the glistening copper-colored shell.

In her anger, it took her a few moments to realize that the rending sounds were dying off, and the humming was fading. She stopped pounding and took a step back.

"Dalisay, are you there?" the senior chief asked, and she realized he'd been trying to contact her for the last minute, ever since she'd flipped the lever.

"I'm here," she said, her mind in a jumble.

"Thank God! I thought . . ."

"I'm OK. What happened?"

"What happened? I'll tell you what happened. You shut down the fucking power just in time. You saved the *Victory!*"

NAVAL HOSPITAL REFUGE

Chapter 5

"Hell, she's still among the living," a familiar voice cut through the fog.

Beth opened her eyes to see Mercy, Turbeville, Fatboy, and the lieutenant standing around her.

"Of course, she is. She's just skating, taking it easy while we do all the work," Mercy said, punching Fatboy in the arm.

"Eat me," Beth said, fighting to clear her head of the cotton that enveloped it. "You lay here with spluge being pumped through you and see how you like it."

Mercy leaned forward and said, "I'd rather I get the spluge pumped into me another way, if you know what I mean. Rock's pretty good at—"

"Mercy!" Beth managed to shout, cutting her sister-in-law off. "I don't need to hear about your gutter games!"

"Just saying, you know," Mercy said, with a sly smile.

The lieutenant, who'd rolled his eyes at Mercy's admittedly crude comment, stepped up and asked, "How are you? I mean, your prognosis? The docs won't release that to us."

Beth looked up at the scrubber that pushed the Triiodinfil, the "spluge," through her. The nasty white substance was supposed to "grab" radiation in her body and remove it where it would be taken out and stored for umpteen thousand years or whatever its half-life would be.

The spluge particles were larger than blood cells, and while they didn't actually hurt as they moved through her body, the process was thoroughly unpleasant. She'd been sedated to better tolerate it, which was making her mind fuzzy.

Still, the fact that she was undergoing it was a good sign. Although, other than her cuts and scrapes, she'd still felt OK on the *Victory*, but she'd absorbed enough radiation that the ship's surgeon had put her under for a more aggressive initial decontamination. She'd been in a medically-induced coma for the transit back and had only been allowed to regain consciousness a few hours ago, a full week after the incident.

"I absorbed something like twenty-three Grays, but they're cleaning me up. I've got another four days of this, and if the readings are OK, I'll be back to full duty."

"Hell, I'd milk it for longer than that. Or you're gonna be giving birth to mutant babies if you ever find a real spluge donor." Mercy said with a raucous laugh, pointing at the scrubber. "See what I did with that?" she asked Fatboy. "A real spluge donor?"

Mercy kept a smile plastered on her face, but she knew it looked forced. Mercy was joking around, but Beth had been worried about just that possibility, and the doctor who'd spoken with her when she awoke hadn't been that reassuring.

Beth had absorbed 23 Grays, or 2300 rads. This was as much as old-fashioned radiation therapy, but over her entire body and not localized with a collimated beam to the specific cancer cells. In the old days of the atomic age, that was a significant dose that could kill within a few weeks. That changed with modern medicine, but while it was no longer lethal, it could still affect the eggs Beth had carried in her ovaries since she was born. Beth had no near-term plans to giving birth, but the thought that she might not be able to someday filled her with dread.

"And . . . hey, you OK?" Mercy asked, seeing the expression on Beth's face.

"Yeah, I'm fine," Beth said, waving a hand in dismissal. "Just uncomfortable. But what's going on out there, I mean with the mine and the *Vickie*? I never found out much before they put me under, and these med folks aren't telling me anything."

"Probably because they don't know," the lieutenant said, looking around to see if anyone was within earshot. "Yeah, it was a mine, one new to us. Only five dead, by some miracle, and the ship was still able to navigate back to the Station. She's heading for the yards for some extensive work, but she'll be back in the fight."

"Only five dead? To be honest, I expected it to be much worse," Beth said.

"Well, we were lucky it hit us where it did," the lieutenant said.

"What? The cyclotron almost wrecked us!" Beth almost shouted.

Lieutenant (JG) Salamanca held up both hands, palms out as if to shush her.

"If it hadn't hit us there, we would've been immediately destroyed. Like the *Courageous*," he said in a whisper.

"The *Courageous*? What happened to her?" Beth asked, a sinking feeling in her belly.

The *Courageous* was part of Operation Urgent Spear, a concurrent operation to free Portland. They were to commence operations simultaneously with Operation Urgent Hammer.

"She evidently hit the same kind of mine. There were no survivors."

Beth stared at him, her mouth dropped open. It took her a moment to process what he'd just said, and not because of the Triiodinfil that coursed through her.

"Yeah, we were lucky," Mercy said, grabbing Beth's hand. "And we were lucky that you were on the *Vickie*. There were still over 500 hundred on board when you shut the cannon down."

"Were you . . . ?"

"We were off. But not everyone was. You saved them," she said earnestly before she broke back into her more usual irreverent self. "But we'll get into that during about a million years of hotwashes. Right now, we're here to celebrate. Are you going to tell her, or am I?" she asked the lieutenant.

"Tell me what?"

"Well, Turbeville here's getting a Gold Star, and you're getting a Platinum Star. It isn't official, yet, but it's a done deal." the lieutenant said.

Beth shrugged. The Navy being the Navy, she'd thought they would award her something, but she hadn't dwelled on it. She already had two Platinum Stars, and a third had to be pretty rare. She was more relieved, however, simply to be alive.

"Satan's nuts! That's not the cool part," Mercy said, cutting in while frowning impatiently at their flight leader. "You're getting the anchor device."

"The anchor? But I'm a fighter pilot."

"And you did your hero shit on a ship. You get an anchor to go along with your prop and crossed rifles. Do you see what I'm getting at?"

"Uh . . . not really."

"You're the first sailor in over fifty years to get the trifecta, and only the third ever."

"Trifecta?"

"Geeze, that spluge must be affecting your brain. The trifecta. Anchor, prop, and rifles. All three Platinum Stars."

Beth looked at the other three, and they all nodded.

"Pretty awesome," Fatboy said.

It *was* awesome, she realized as it sunk in. Her Order of Honor was a higher medal, of course, but to think that only three sailors in history had this *trifecta*? Beth didn't chase medals, but still, she felt pretty good about that. Given time, she'd feel proud.

"Are you still here?" one of the ward nurses asked as she breezed into the room. "I told you ten minutes. We need to take NSP2 Dalisay to the lab now for readings."

"Hey, we'll come back and check on you. We're under a stand-down now until the stars figure out what's next," Mercy said.

She leaned in and gave her a kiss. The others shook her hand before they turned to leave as a corpsman guided in a gurney.

"Hey, D'Andre," Beth said, stopping Turbeville.

"I've got a callsign for you. Hodar."

He looked confused and asked, "Hodar?"

"Yeah. It's from a character in one of the literature classics, a fantasy. The name Hodar comes from 'Hold the door.' He held shut a door from a bunch of undead, allowing a future king to escape. You didn't hold a door, but you went down there with me, and you jacked up the conduit so I could get through. Hodar."

The young pilot contemplated that for a moment before a smile broke out on his face. "I like that."

"You lucky son-of-a-bitch," Mercy said, clapping him on the shoulder. "I was about to christen you Asswipe."

SIERRA STATION

Chapter 6

Beth almost skipped down the passage to the squadron spaces. She was glad to get out of the hospital, glad to no longer have the Triiodinfil pumped through her body (she couldn't use the "spluge" nickname anymore, even in her thoughts. It was too disgusting).

She'd been given a clean bill of health . . . almost. Her body was free of radiation, and damage to her cells had been minimal. She'd have to undergo annual testing, and there was a slight increase in the chance of getting glaucoma sometime in the future, but the docs didn't think she was at particular risk of cancer or anemia. There was still concern about her eggs, however. Two had been removed and examined. There was evidence of mitochondrial damage, but none of the doctors could give her a firm answer on whether that would affect any future children. For all of medical science's advances over the millennia, nature still withheld some mysteries.

Beth had tried to push that out of her mind, but with limited success. Lying in bed while getting pumped with Triiodinfil left her with little else to do but think, and even for someone who had never really contemplated having kids, the thought pushed her into depression. Still, she was lucky, and she knew it. She was alive and no worse for wear. Two weeks after the incident, she was back on flight status.

The threat of radiation exposure had been less than she had been led to believe. Not the threat of death, but by radiation. The cyclotron breaking apart while the protons were whizzing around would have still destroyed the ship, just not by radiation. That would have just been the icing on the cake, "Scouring clean the debris," as one of her radiation techs at the naval hospital described it.

"Hey, Fire Ant, welcome back," Possum, one of the warrant officer pilots said as they passed each other in the passage. "You doing OK?"

"Fit as a fiddle," Beth said. "Just going to the hangar to check on the *Tala*."

"And only *then* check in with the CO, I gather?"

Beth smiled and said, "Gotta know if my ride's combat-ready."

"Like a true fighter-jock. Not that we're getting released anytime soon," Possum said. "Hey, I don't know if the CO's got anything planned, but I know a bunch of us want to hear your side of what happened. Hodar gave us his side during the hotwash, but you know . . ."

Beth smiled. She wasn't sure "Hodar" would catch on, especially as the reference was an obscure one. But Possum just used Turbeville's callsign as if it was a done deal.

"Sure. I can give you my side. It really wasn't much, just flipping a switch, but if there's nothing planned, buy me a San Miguel, and I'll keep talking as long as the beer's flowing."

"You got yourself a deal!" Possum said, his face breaking out into a smile before continuing the other way.

Beth stood there a moment, just watching the pilot walk away. When she first joined the squadron, she'd been shunned as a civilian pilot, brought into the Stingers for some PC reasoning. Mercy had been her only real friend in the beginning, but over time, she'd become accepted, and her circle of friends had gotten bigger.

Still, for her to be able to just chat with others like Possum with whom she wasn't particularly close, to even put the warrant officer on the line for a beer, well, the old Floribeth Salinas O'Shea Dalisay would never have been able to do that.

Beth liked the new Floribeth better.

She turned back and continued to the hangar, feeling better than she had for a week.

As she expected, Josh was on his back and under the *Tala*, working on something, as she crossed the hangar deck to reach her fighter. She swore her plane captain would sleep inside the *Tala* if he could. If someone could fall in love with an inanimate object, it would be Josh. She knew that he considered himself the true "owner" of the *Tala*, merely lending it to her when she had to take it out.

"Everything OK?" she asked, more just for social graces, as she bent over to see what he was doing.

She long ago ceased to worry that there was anything really wrong when he was working on her fighter. He just couldn't keep away from her, and Beth was all for that. Not every plane captain was so dedicated to their fighter.

"Oh, hi. Glad you're back," he said, pulling himself out from under the *Tala*. "I just wanted to check the response deltas for the P-five-oh-threes. I thought I noticed a slight surge along the condenser coupling . . ."

Beth just nodded as if she understood what he was saying. Beth flew the *Tala* into harm's way, but she couldn't recognize a P-503 if she was slapped across the face with it. She didn't have to know what it was. It was enough that Josh did. Still, she put a serious look on her face and tried to look like she was following him.

He paused for a breath, and Beth cut in. "So, what's the story? What's our new ship?"

"You haven't heard?"

"I just got off the shuttle from Refuge, and I came here first."

Josh nodded. He would have done the same thing.

"We just got the word. We're on the *Bobolink*."

Beth frowned, then said, "That doesn't sound like a battlecruiser."

"That's because it isn't. It's a corvette. *Kestral* class."

Beth's frown deepened. Despite being in the Navy, she wasn't up on all the classes of ships, but she remembered that corvettes were the next size down from destroyers.

"But we can't fit the squadron on a corvette, right?"

Josh laughed, then said, "Not even close. It's going to be tough to shoehorn in just the eight of us."

"Eight?"

"Yeah. Fox and Echo Flights. Lieutenant Hsu's the detachment commander."

Josh was a brilliant plane captain, but he sometimes missed the ball on simple communications.

"OK, Josh. Wait. Fox and Echo are being detached to a corvette. Why? Are we going on some independent mission? What's going on?"

The plane captain wrinkled his brows for a moment, then carefully said, "The FALs like bigger ships to target. At least that's what all the AIs determined after the last few battles were analyzed. So, the admiralty wants us to go in smaller. And if a mine takes out one of us, we're still combat-capable. All of the Wasps are being parceled out, not just us."

"Wait. They only target the bigger ships? That's not right. I've fought crystal fighters before, and they sure the hell weren't ignoring me as too small."

"But there weren't any capital ships then, right?" he asked.

She paused a moment, then realized he was right. The Navy hadn't wanted to risk the big ships until they knew what they faced. And in the battle of Retribution, they had first targeted the *Chon Buri*, which wasn't much of a threat to them, but was bigger than anything else the humans had.

That was a lot of assuming, though, Beth thought. Even if it was true, the crystals had proven to be adaptable before, changing tactics to meet the human threat. She wasn't sure that putting all their eggs into the "big ship" basket was that great of an idea. All of that was way above her pay grade, however. If the powers-that-be wanted to put eight Wasps in a corvette, she'd salute smartly and march on.

RS BOBOLINK

Chapter 7

Beth turned her face to the cone, feeling the dirt and grime flake away. She wasn't a fan of sonic showers. They made her skin crawl as if she was covered by a million ants. But with strict water rationing on the *Bobo*, water showers were a thing of the past.

That had never been the case with the *Victory*. That ship was designed for supporting a huge crew. The *Bobolink* was not. Heavily automated, she normally put to space with a crew of 32. With the two flights squeezed in, that added 21 more bodies—bodies that had to be fed, given a rack upon which to sleep, and all the requirements of daily life.

And this was a small detachment for eight Wasps: eight pilots, eight plane captains, and five support techs. The TO called for 33 people to support two flights on independent ops.

"Hey, Fire Ant, you done?" Lieutenant Morton "Chipshot" Hsu shouted. "We're waiting."

With a sigh, Beth turned off the shower. She might not like the thing, but she hated smelling herself more. Not just her. All her fellow shipmates.

She wrapped the towel around her, making sure it was secure, and stepped out of the single shower assigned to the two flights. Five people were in line waiting to use it.

Beth's towel covered most of her petite body. Not so with Chipshot. A full lieutenant and the senior pilot aboard, he was younger than her, but his body was already getting heavy around the belly, and his towel, hastily wrapped around his waist, looked about ready to fall off. Beth sucked in her own belly as she turned to slide past him to get back to their berthing, but still, she got a face full of Chipshot as he pushed past her and into the tiny shower.

The close quarters sucked. Beth had been spoiled since hitting the fleet. Sierra Station had never been at capacity, and the *Victory* had more than enough spaces that as a pilot, she'd only shared her quarters with Mercy. Now, the eight pilots shared a tiny berthing space designed for four. That meant hot-racking it. Beth and Mercy shared the top bunk on the starboard side. Technically, that meant Beth had it for 12 hours, and Mercy had it for the following 12 hours. For some of the others, that rule held firm. For the two sisters-in-law, they were both small and not averse to sharing the rack at the same time.

Even sharing the rack, however, did little to alleviate the crowding and sense of claustrophobia. Beth didn't think she was a prude. She was more conservative than Mercy, sure, but she thought she was pretty open about most things. But she was having a hard time adjusting to living in each other's laps—the farting, burping, body odor, nudity, and constant chatter from the others. And there was only one way to get away from it all—getting out in the *Tala* where she could have some blessed privacy.

The problem with that, however, was that in the last week since boarding the *Bobolink*, she'd been out only three times, and that only to practice launch and recovery. There had been no flights of any length of time.

She entered their berthing. The four racks were occupied by sleepers, and the racks wouldn't turn over for another hour. Beth pulled out a clean set of pilot blues, dropped the towel, and quickly slipped into them. The first time she'd changed in this berthing, she'd pulled her overalls on over her towel, then pulled the towel out, just like she'd always done at home on New Cebu, but Chipshot and Tiger—Lieutenant (JG) Constance Ronuldson—had laughed at her. It wasn't that she was shy—OK, maybe a little—but that was just how people did it back home. But they'd teased her about it, so, now she made an effort to show them she didn't care.

Still, she was glad the two were still at the shower.

She stood there a moment, wondering what to do for the next hour. She'd already eaten before taking her shower, and their shift was officially on free time. The recreational facilities aboard the *Bobolink* were sorely lacking, however. She could stream any of a zillion or two shows, but she usually watched with Mercy. What she really wanted to do was just to veg out, maybe take a nap.

She climbed up on Hodar/the lieutenant's bunk, hanging on with her hands on the edge of hers and Mercy's bunk to look at her. She was asleep, softly snoring.

"Mercy," she whispered. When her sister-in-law didn't respond, she whispered it a little louder.

Nothing.

Holding on tightly with her left hand, she reached out with her right and gave Mercy a nudge on the thigh. Mercy stirred, then opened one eye.

"Oh, you're awake," Beth said. "Just checking. Mind if I join you?"

Mercy mumbled something unintelligible, then scooted a few centimeters over toward the bulkhead. Beth took that as a yes. Using the two steps they'd had one of the crew weld onto the bulkhead at the foot of the rack, she climbed in, her feet toward Mercy's head.

It was tight. Even as small as the two were, the racks were made for one, and that with an economy of space at the forefront of the design engineers. Beth shifted her body, slowly nudging Mercy farther to the bulkhead until she had enough space to lay down.

Then, just as all military since the time of the Phoenicians had done whenever they had a free moment, Beth fell asleep.

Chapter 8

A full month later, Beth was in the *Tala*, ready to launch for real—and not a moment too soon. Mercy was under the impression that the admiralty forced them into such tight quarters and let them stew so they'd be good and angry when they were thrust back into combat.

Beth wouldn't put it past them, but the official word was that the fleet needed to work out an entirely new way of fighting. Coupled with the still yet unknown mine threat and the fact that there wasn't any reported massive genocide on the captive planets, it made sense that the planners needed more time.

That time was eroding their readiness, though. Tempers had been flaring. Mercy was not speaking to Chipshot, and the two flight leaders were at odds that they couldn't hide from the rest. The *Bobolink* didn't have simulators like the *Victory* did, and training flights had been curtailed.

Beth patted her console, glad to finally be getting out of the ship. The *Tala* even smelled cleaner.

"Foxtrot-Three, five minutes," the launch captain told her.

Beth rapped on her canopy, but Josh already heard. He gave her a thumbs up, passed, "Get some," on the S2S, then hopped off the nose. He wouldn't be able to watch the launch and had to get out of the hangar/cargo bay.

The *Victory* launched Wasps along a magnetic rail, the control of each fighter only passing to the pilot after 10,000 klicks. The distance was overkill, but the less the ship had to absorb the fighter's engine exhaust the better.

The *Bobolink* didn't have launch rails, so each Wasp had to leave the makeshift hangar under its own power as if they were on a planet's surface. But planets generally had an atmosphere which buffered some of their exhaust. The *Bobolink* didn't have that protection. So, sailors did what they've always done: they improvised.

Four deck hands in EVA suits trundled up a cargo mule—not the aviation tillies normally used in flight ops, but the same ones that moved pallets of food and supplies. This mule had its forks modified to match the Wasps, handling points.

Josh would be watching from outside the hangar, and Beth knew that must be killing him as the crew positioned the mule, and a moment later, lifted the *Tala*. All her displays were green, so they hadn't screwed up anything . . . yet.

The *Tala* lurched as they started forward, carrying her past Hodar, who gave her a thumbs up, then slowing down slightly as they carefully maneuvered her into the cargo lock. Two of the handlers climbed on top of the *Tala*, and for a moment, Beth felt protective, wanting to tell them to get the hell off.

The normal inner cargo hold lock was not large enough for a Wasp, so it had to be modified. The *Tala* barely fit, and Beth held her breath as the inner door slowly closed. She thought it was going to clip her fighter, and she had to hold herself back, fighting the urge to yell at the deck chief to stop. The two deckhands on top of the *Tala* eyeballed it closed, though.

"Depressurizing, Foxtrot-Three," launch control informed her.

She couldn't tell much from inside the *Tala*, but the EVA suits on the deckhands puffed out. One of them scooted up to the canopy, put his face close, and looked in. Beth had an urge to give him the finger. She had no idea where that came from, but it was always best to stay on good terms with the sailors whose job it was to safely launch and recover her. She smiled instead and gave him a thumbs up.

"Outer lock doors opening."

It seemed to take forever, but finally, the door was open, and Beth could see into space. The deckhands slid off the *Tala*, hooked up the cable, then clambered back over her to get on the inside. With another lurch, the *Tala* started moving out of the ship down some makeshift—and static—rails. They'd been welded on, giving a platform upon which the *Tala* would sit. "Sit" with the aid of magnets, that held her traction plate. As the *Tala* moved outside of the ship, she passed beyond the *Bobolink's* artificial gravity.

"We've got you locked, Foxtrot Three. Do not engage engines until I give you clearance."

I know, I know, Beth thought. *You don't want me frying the two deckhands.*

Behind her, the outer door was closing. It was built tough, and it should be more than able to withstand the *Tala's* exhaust given how little power she would use to move away from the ship.

She craned her head back to watch the door, and as it closed, launch control said, "Foxtrot-Three, you are being disengaged and are cleared to launch. You are not authorized to exceed zero-point-zero-two percent of thrust until cleared."

"Roger that."

"Fly safe," the voice said softly, sounding human for once.

Beth activated her engine and powered up. Slowly, she took the *Tala* away from the ship. It didn't matter how slow it was, though. She was in her fighter, ready to close with the crystals. After over a month of enforced activity, it was time to kick some ass.

****

Beth took another long swallow from Dispenser 6. She knew she should cut back, to ration herself, but she'd never been too good at doing that. She was just grateful that Josh had managed to find the Coke on the *Bobolink*.

It had taken an excruciatingly long amount of time to get just the eight Wasps on the *Bobolink* launched. On the *Victory*, two squadrons could be launched in 20 minutes. On the *Bobolink*, the eight fighters had taken over an hour.

But now, the different flights had converged. She couldn't directly see any of the other fighters, of course, but her combat display looked good with the entire squadron moving to the last gate into the Portland system.

As they had never made it that far in the previous attempt to free the planet, the combat planners hadn't changed the initial plan by much. Yes, the Marines were being transported by a fleet of smaller vessels, and there was nothing larger than a monitor in the initial wave, but the big arrows were the same.

"You ready to kick some FAL ass?" Mercy passed on the S2S.

"You'd better believe it, sista mine. Portland is going to be ours again."

I hope the Portlandiers will be, too.

In their briefs, the possibility was raised that the crystals might take revenge on the humans when they started to lose the planet. The Stinger's secondary mission was to intercede if that happened. They would shift from supporting the Marines to try and save the civilian populace. Beth hoped it wouldn't get to that, but her gut told her it was a very real possibility. The crystals had wiped out three planets so far, after all. What was one more human world to them?

"Stingers, I just wanted to give you an update before we jump the gate. Task Force Sixty-seven has just engaged the crystals. There is a single hive ship," the CO passed, using the term for the large component ships that had come into favor. "Our mission remains the same. We're to get the Marines down to the surface of the planet, so your original orders are still in effect."

"Lucky bastards," Mercy passed on the S2S.

She'd made known her feelings quite explicitly. With five kills and making ace, Mercy wanted to go head-to-head with the crystal fighters to add to her total. Beth understood the desire, but her recent brush with death and the knowledge that she may never be able to have children had given her time for retrospection, and the result had shifted her opinion just a bit. That could be dangerous for a fighter pilot who had to act aggressively if she wanted to survive, but she was confident in her capabilities. The hard truth, however, was that her best friend wasn't as good a pilot as she was, and Mercy was lucky to still be alive. Beth was afraid she was living on borrowed time. Beth didn't want to lose her, so if this mission was going to be a little less dangerous, Beth was fine with that.

Could be a little less dangerous, she corrected herself. *No one knows what's going to happen.*

"Just keep focusing on our mission, Mercy," Beth said. "The Marines need us."

"I know, but I need to splash another FAL."

"You may get the chance. Just keep your panties on."

"You know me, sista. I'm flying commando."

Beth bit back a laugh and tried to think of a rejoinder when the control of her Wasp reverted to the CO's. Shooting a gate so tightly was done more effectively under a single AI. Beth hated it even more than being under launch control. There, she was being spat out into the void. With a gate, she was converging with 52 other Wasps to pass through a small gate. A collision at these speeds would ruin anyone's day.

She watched her display in silence as the ships converged together, adjusting the scale as they got closer and closer to the gate. But the CO's AI was more than capable, and the *Tala* shot the gate, and they were in the Portland system.

Immediately, her display lit up. The hive ship was spewing off fighters to meet TF-67. Five monitors, their huge hadron cannons blazing, were peppering the big ship, but they were barely ablating the thing, destroying the component fighters, but not the combined ship itself. That had been expected. The monitors were only there to fix the big ship in place for the real effort.

Beth tore herself away from the battle. As the *Tala* reverted to her control, she had to focus on her own mission. Within minutes, the Marines would start shooting the gate, hundreds of small, unarmed shuttles with Marines packed like sardines inside. The Marines had been rehearsing non-stop, but this was still the first time they'd ever attempted a planetary landing from what was essentially an old-fashioned landing craft and without their troop carriers' big ground-support guns.

Those troop carriers and their guns would arrive, but not until the space was swept for mines. For all Beth knew, she could be blasting past a hundred of them right now, only safe because she was considered too small to be a threat.

Twenty-six huge ships, likely ore carriers, were in orbit around Portland. From the data collected by the scouts and drones, these looked to be inert, huge shells. When filled, small craft, indiscernible from the crystal fighters, attached themselves to the bigger hulks and became the power source to take them wherever. Five had already left the system since the planet was taken over, which was fewer than the experts had predicted.

As the squadron took up their course toward the planet, crystals rose up from the surface. It didn't take long for the battle AIs to determine that they were heading to meet the Stingers and Exemplars.

"Looks like you're going to get your shot, Mercy," Beth passed, her voice determined. "We need to keep them off the Marines."

Beth might have been willing to accept a less active role, but with the threat coming to meet them, her sense of duty was too strong to ignore. More than that, even with her brush with mortality, she had a warrior's blood coursing through her veins, and that could never be denied.

The commander's AI fed in their individual courses. The two forces would reach reasonable torpedo range in another two hours, and that was a long time to stew. The Wasps could fire their own hadron cannons now, but they'd never proven to be overly effective against the crystal ships, so this was going to be torpedoes and rail guns—in other words, this was going to be a close-in rumble.

She took another sip of the Coke, draining the dispenser dry, and immediately regretting it. She should have had more discipline.

With time on her hands, she turned back to the bigger battle taking place. One of the monitors, which was little more than power and armor, was out of action. three of the remaining four continued to fire into the hive ship, sweeping off crystal fighters like a loofa sweeping off new skin. But just like a loofa, all that did was reveal new fighters just underneath.

VF-48 and VF-105 from TF-67 were closing in to meet the crystal fighters. They were already taking heavy casualties. VF-48, the Lightning Bolts, was down to 54%.

This was all part of the plan. They had to focus the crystals' attention for the hammer strike. Beth had to wonder about the admiralty. How could anyone order pilots into a chainsaw like that when they weren't expected to actually succeed?

The hive ship seemed to be cooperating. More and more crystal fighters were peeling off of it and rushing into the fight. That was a good thing, but it also meant more Wasps were being splashed.

"Stinger, stand by to assume VF-48's mission," the CO passed.

"What about the Marines?" Hodar asked on the flight net. "They'll be sitting ducks for those crystals coming at us."

"Nothing's changed yet. Just be ready in case it does," the lieutenant said, calming the young pilot down.

"Where is it?" Mercy asked Beth. "It should have arrived by now."

"Maybe problems. This is experimental, after all," Beth said.

"The sims worked."

"And those are sims. Not real life," Beth snapped.

Which wasn't fair. It wasn't Mercy's fault that the Navy's latest and greatest had evidently failed. Good pilots had died setting the table, and now—

Before she could finish the thought, her alarm sounded three times. Fifteen seconds later, God's own rocket passed through the gate, traveling at .97 C.

When Commander Tuominen had hit and destroyed the hive ship, he'd G-shot to 80 Gs and had hit at .64 C. Even with a small Wasp, that was an enormous force, enough to destroy the ship.

This hive ship had to have known what had happened and would have taken some precautions. The only way around that was to hit this one at a higher speed. But how to achieve that.

The answer was with an unmanned Wasp, which could accelerate at 121.3 Gs. Fast, but almost impossible to turn around. If something coming that fast missed the target, it would take forever for it to come back for another pass. Not just turning around. It was not very maneuverable, and it could be dodged when it was first detected.

So, how to get a hyper-missile like this to hit? Reduce the distance so the target can't dodge.

But it took a long time to accelerate to the desired speed.

The answer was relatively easy in theory, even if difficult in practice. The weaponized Wasp, or in this case, two of them, did their acceleration on the other side of a gate, and the monitors and Wasps on the business side of the gate had to nudge and maneuver the hiveship so that one of these Wasps could hit it immediately upon shooting the gate.

Fourteen seconds after shooting the gate, the first Wasp slammed into the crystal hive ship. The blast was so bright that the *Tala's* canopy couldn't dim in time, and Beth winced in the harsh light.

A moment later, the back-up Wasp shot the gate. There was no longer a target, and it simply continued on out of the system.

"Get some!" Mercy shouted on the S2S as the net erupted in shouts.

Beth clenched her fist and hit the top of her canopy. She'd doubted the plan, but it had worked. Not without a heavy cost, however. Only two of the unmanned monitors were left, and they would now turn toward the planet. But 83 Wasps had been destroyed, 83 fighters with a human aboard. Most of them would be dead.

Compared with the masses on the planet, that was nothing, but as a Navy pilot, Beth felt the loss. She just had to make sure their losses were not in vain.

The hive ship might be gone, but that didn't mean the planet was undefended. There were still hundreds of crystal fighters swarming to meet them, and there were tens of thousands of them on the planet that the Marines were going to have to defeat before the humans on Portland would be safe again.

"We still have our mission," the CO passed on the squadron net. "The hive ship was just the first battle here, but the war isn't won yet."

Beth focused her attention on the developing battle situation. The CO's battle AI was constantly analyzing the data, trying to determine the crystals most probably course of action, and then the best response to meet it.

"Marines are in system," Lieutenant (JG) Salamanca passed.

On her display, a mass of green icons were winking into the system. This was why the Stingers were there. The Navy might have massive weapons, but even after thousands of years, it still took ground troops to take and hold terrain. The Stingers had to make sure the Marines got on the ground so they could do what they did so well. Beth made a silent vow to herself to make sure no crystal fighter got close to the grunts.

She was still a little far out, and they'd not been cleared to fire yet, but she armed her torps. The M-57 had proven to be the most successful weapon to use against the crystals, and Beth was itching to fire them.

"You're not cleared to fire yet, Fire Ant," the lieutenant said, noting the arming.

"Roger that. But the new circuits sometimes take a few tries to arm, and I want to be ready.

There was silence on the net for a few moments, then one after the other, Mercy, Hodar, and the lieutenant armed theirs. Beth had to suppress a smile. The *Tala* was not tied into the rest of the Wasps, so, Beth couldn't see what they were doing, but she wouldn't be too surprised if they were arming now, too. There was a tiny chance that a torp would fire when it armed, but there was a far greater chance that the balky arming hardware would delay, and a fighter could need a torpedo and not have one ready to use.

She turned her attention back to the incoming crystals. They were still closing, 45 minutes from the optimum firing window. Soon, their fight would commence, the lives of 60,000 Marines, and through them, 20,000,000 civilians on the ground, were at stake.

"You ready for this?" Beth asked Mercy on the S2S.

"Satan's nuts, I was born ready. Let the suckers come!" Mercy said, her voice filled with excitement.

Beth turned to look where she knew Mercy and the *Louhi* were flying, more by instinct than as if she could actually spot her best friend. Mercy sounded too excited, which could be a bad thing when making cooler decisions could be the difference between splashing a FAL or getting splashed by one.

"Just be smart," Beth said.

"Don't worry. I ain't gonna make any mistakes. I just need a couple more of them to add to my tally."

Beth knew that Mercy was obsessed with her kill total. Beth also thought Mercy was lucky to still be alive, and she feared that Mercy would push too hard to get that next kill, and that would leave her vulnerable. And so, breaking all sorts of promises to first Commander Tuominen, then to Commander Vander Beek, that she would treat Mercy as any other wingman, she decided that she'd have to keep an extra vigilant eye on her as well as her own situation.

I'd do it for any wingman, she told herself, not quite convincingly.

First thing I've gotta do is pay attention to the FALs.

She was still being positioned by the commander's AI, but she'd be released as soon as the battle commenced. It wasn't that she didn't trust the other AI, but she'd be stupid to rely on it when she might be able to discern something about them on her own that could give her an edge.

She zeroed her display to the advancing fighters, and so focused was she on the crystals that she didn't notice what was happening to the planet until Mercy said, "What the fuck is happening to Portland?"

Beth frowned and shifted her display to encompass the planet . . . and it *shimmered*, if that was the right word, for a moment. *Shuddered?* But how could a planet shudder?

She reset her display, but that didn't help. The planet looked slightly off.

"Scooter, do we have any—" Beth started to ask the lieutenant until cut off by an intense flash of light that momentarily blinded her display.

When her display corrected, Portland wasn't there, at least as it was supposed to be. An expanding ball of what looked to be flaming gas was in its place.

The *Tala's* alarms went off, the CO's voice broke through to order, "All hands, break, break, break, break. Rochester. I say again, Rochester. Divert all auxiliary power to your Paxtons."

Beth was acting before she even realized what was happening. "Rochester" was the emergency code to return immediately to the gate and exit the system. The Paxton Repellers, coupled with the fighter's auto-avoid kept the *Tala* from impacts with micro-up-to-300-kg space objects. Anything larger, and the Beth was expected to simply avoid them. The downside was that they diverted power and scanner capability to the repellers.

In this case, a necessary trade-off.

A Wasp was extremely maneuverable, but it couldn't turn on a dime. The laws of physics could not be contravened. Beth poured power into the turn, but the *Tala* still had forward momentum that was taking her ever closer to the planet, or what had once been a planet.

She refused to consider what had happened. She knew that would make her numb, and if she wanted to live, she had to be in control.

"Mercy, you with me?" she asked, fighting the G's as the *Tala* tried to swing around in a 180.

"On your ass. What the fuck happened?"

"Just focus, sista."

The expanding ball of gas? Rubble? Planet? reached out, sucking in the still accelerating tail-end Charlies of the FAL fighters heading their way. One by one, each was swallowed up. All the while, the Stingers were trying to reverse course before that ball reached them.

Beth ran some quick calculations. The numbers weren't good. The *Tala* was turning, no longer heading directly toward the Portland, but the cloud was expanding in all directions, including into her projected course. By the time she would be heading back, the remains of the planet (and 20 million people, she tried to suppress for the moment), would engulf her. Not just her, but probably the first four flights as well.

She was just about to relay that to the CO when the order came, "Echo, Fox, Golf, and Bravo, initiate G-shot."

Beth hated G-shot with a passion. Most pilots never initiated the process after flight school, and this would be her fourth time. Yet, she didn't hesitate. She pulled up the safety cover and manually hit the red button. Almost immediately, G-shot flooded her body, the pain as bad as she'd remembered, and she could feel her arteries thicken up. The docs said that was impossible, but Beth knew what she felt.

The *Tala* immediately increased the power, almost counter-intuitively increasing the closing speed to the expanding cloud of what had been Portland. But she was also turning tighter, right at the limits of what the human body, even under G-shot, could survive. Beth's visions grayed on the edges, and it took an effort of will to shift her display back to the squadron disposition. All of the Wasps were in the process of reversing course, but she keyed on the *Louhi* first, then the rest of her flight.

There was no sign of the crystal fighters, but they were no longer the main threat, anyway. The threat was the very planet they'd come to rescue.

G-shot interfered with the thought process, so, it was easier not to think of the people for the moment. The planet had become a faceless enemy, one that they had to avoid. She was cognizant enough to run some simulations, and it looked close. The *Tala's* sensor could now pick up some individual chunks of what had been an inhabited planet, chunks large enough and traveling fast enough that they would smash the *Tala* if they hit her.

Finally, she was no longer approaching the planet, having come around 90 degrees. But the danger wasn't over. She might not be approaching, and she was slowly coming around tighter and moving away, but the cloud wasn't slowing down. The *Tala's* speed was greater than that of the cloud, but she was still oblique to it. Beth wouldn't be safe until her separation rate exceeded the cloud's rate of expansion.

There wasn't much Beth and the others could do but trust their fighters and ride it out. She kept an eye on the other Wasps and the expanding cloud, which kept reaching out to them, but the closing speed slowing down as the Wasps pulled tighter into their turns.

G-shot also affected the sense of time. It had to be only ten or twenty minutes, but it seemed like hours before the edge of the cloud started to recede, never quite reaching fourteen of the most threatened Wasps, including Beth and the *Tala*. She'd come within a couple of hundred klicks, which was a whisper-thin buffer in the vast reaches of space, before she began to gain separation. The leading edge of the cloud kissed two of the Bravo Wasps, but they managed to emerge intact after a couple of minutes.

Beth didn't wait for the order. She was safe now, the *Tala* able to outrun the cloud back to the gate. She cut G-shot, wincing as it was purged from her system. Nauseous and achy, her brain came back to full functionality.

Her personal threat passed, what had just happened hit her, and hit her hard. She threw up into her helmet and whipped it off, heaving out the Coke first, then switching to dry heaves.

When the FALs lost their hive ship, they knew they were going to lose the planet. Instead of letting that happen, they destroyed it.

Chapter 9

"What the fuck! I told you to keep your god-damned feet off my rack!" Chipshot shouted, pulling Tiger off of the top rack to thud on the deck.

"How the hell am I supposed to get into my rack, then, you piss-donk!" Tiger shouted back, coming to her feet with a hard shove to Chipshot's chest.

"I don't give a shit. Fly if you fucking have to," Chipshot shouted, coming in to shove Tiger back, who twisted aside at the last moment and wrapped an arm around her flight leader and wingman's neck and riding him down into Hodar's bunk, waking the young pilot up from a deep sleep.

Beth had been lying in bed, her thoughts drifting into the crazy half-asleep, half-awake world where nothing made sense . . . and Tiger and Chipshot, two best buddies, fighting made no sense, either. It took her a moment to realize that this was reality. She jumped out of her rack, her feet grazing Tiger's back as she fell, where she struggled with Hodar to separate the two.

"Stop this shit!" she screamed, arm around Tiger's neck and she strained to pull them apart. "You're wingmates, for God's sake!"

"He's a fucking asshole," Tiger said, not willing to give up her headlock.

"He's your friend!" Beth shouted, pulling harder. "It's just this damned situation, and you know it. Our nerves are fried."

Beth might be small, but her hold was tight, and she was cutting off Tiger's air. She knew Tiger might turn on her, and if she did, Beth was dead meat. She just had to hope that rationality would take over.

Finally, Tiger had to breathe, and she loosened her headlock on Chipshot and pulled Beth's arm off from around her neck. Chipshot started to swarm up, murder in his eyes, but Hodar had him wrapped up pretty well.

"Look at you two. You're wingmates, and good friends to boot. You're not the enemies here. It's the FALs, not us! They blew up Portland, not us. Get control of yourselves, for God's sake!"

The two glared at each other for a long moment, chests heaving. Tiger had a mark on the side of her face that was growing red.

"He needs to apologize," she spat out.

"Apologize!" Beth told Chipshot.

"Fucking A, no! I told her not to step on my rack!"

Tiger started to move forward again, but Beth held her back. She was half Tiger's size, but the pilot stopped, glaring over Beth's head at Chipshot.

Once Beth was sure Tiger wasn't going into attack mode, she turned to Chipshot, ignoring the fact that he was an officer and the senior pilot aboard as her own anger and frustration boiled over.

"How the hell is she supposed to get into her rack? Jump? You're being an asshole, Morton," she said, skipping his callsign. She reached up and grabbed him by the collar, then pulled him down until her face was centimeters from his and said, her voice hard, "This sucks. It really sucks. And that's ripping us apart. We don't know what's happening, and flying square circles in this God-forgotten section of nothing isn't helping."

Everything Beth had just said was true. Once the Wasps had been recovered aboard the *Bobolink*, the ship had been sent to sit in space while the brass and government analyzed what happened. Beth knew what happened. The crystals were sending them a message. Try and take back a planet, and they'd destroy it. Simple as that.

And it was effective. The Navy was on a standdown, and there had not been any human attempts to fight the FALs for two months now, two months that a crowded, frustrated crew aboard the *Bobolink* couldn't handle. Fights were a daily occurrence. Several of the ship's crew and even one of the pilots had been busted down a rank by the ship's captain. Pilots! Beth had never heard of a pilot receiving captain's mast during her time in uniform.

Beth—and the rest of the pilots—knew that they were not at fault for the loss of Portland. But knowing that and *feeling* that were two different things. Beth felt guilty, and she kept going over what happened in her mind, wondering what she could have done to change the outcome.

She wasn't the only one. That feeling of guilt, coupled with depression, boredom, crowded conditions, and most of all, not being able to fight back, was a caldron waiting to boil over. Beth was surprised that things hadn't broken down worse. But their reactions pissed Beth off to no end. They were the Navy of Humankind, and if they couldn't band together, then what hope did humanity have?

She was pissed, and that anger was now focused on the two Echo pilots.

"But I don't give a flying fuck if your two petty feelings are hurt," she said. "I don't give a flying fuck if we're parked out here in the black, waiting to do something. I *do* care that you're letting the FALs break the two of you apart. You think you have it rough? How about the twenty million on Portland? How about them?

"You two better start acting like professionals, or so help me . . ."

Beth kept her eyes locked on Chipshot for a long moment, then shifted to Tiger, saying, "Well? What's it gonna be?"

Tiger started to say something, then stopped. She shrugged and stepped back to the two starboard racks and sat at the foot of Chipshot's, waiting to see his response.

Beth turned to him and repeated, "Well?"

He looked down at the deck and mumbled out a soft "I just . . . ah, forget it. Sorry."

He didn't sound too sorry, but Beth wasn't going to push it.

The hatch swung open and a laughing Mercy and Nose came in, ready to claim their turn in the racks. The tensions in the space were still palpable, and the two stopped in their tracks, looking around at the four of them.

"What's going on? Is everything OK?" Mercy asked.

"Everything's fine," Beth answered for the other three.

It was probably fine—for the moment, at least. But if they didn't get back into the fight soon, she was afraid they would tear the ship apart, saving the crystals the trouble.

Chapter 10

"Where do you think we're going?" Mercy asked, which, of course, was the question on everyone's mind.

Beth shrugged. After six weeks on station, the *Bobolink* was on the move. To where, none of the crew or the two Wasp flights knew. The captain hadn't passed that information, and rumors were rampant. They were attacking the crystal homeworld, the crystals were attacking Earth, there was a truce, the war had just escalated into a massive, all-out battle. The most outlandish rumor was that humans and crystals had just formed an alliance against yet another alien race that was pushing into this corner of the galaxy.

Beth didn't have a clue more than anyone else, and instead of going into guessing mode, she just kept her mouth closed. They'd all find out soon enough. Chipshot, as the senior pilot of the eight, had left to try and find out what was happening, and the other seven, along with five of their plane captains, were crowded in the tiny berthing space, waiting for the word.

"I guess anything's better than this shit," Mercy said when Beth didn't answer.

The two of them, along with Josh, were sitting on their rack. From their vantage point, Beth could see the top of Lieutenant (JG's) Salamanca's head—Beth, being four-foot-eight, almost never saw the top of anyone's head. He was young, only 22, but he was already going bald at the crown. Baldness had not been bred out of the human genome, but it was easily treatable, and Beth wondered if her flight leader even realized what was happening to him. For a moment, she was tempted to lean over the edge of her rack and tell him.

What the heck, Floribeth? Now's not the time, if it ever will be. Forget it.

She leaned back when the berthing space loudspeaker crackled to life, and a voice asked, "NSP2 Dalisay, your presence is required in the CIC. Please acknowledge."

Eleven sets of eyes rotated as one to her, and she stammered out, "Uh . . . roger that. I'm on my way."

She could feel their combined gaze burn into her with the force of a hadron cannon as she slid off the bunk, stepping on Hodar's leg on the lower rack for a moment as she sought purchase before a final step to the deck.

"What's going on, Fire Ant?" the lieutenant asked.

"Yeah, what?" Tiger chimed in.

"I don't know," Beth said, feeling self-conscious.

She didn't know, nor could she figure out any reason why she was being ordered to the *Bobolink's* CIC, the heartbeat of the ship's operations.

"I'm going with you," Salamanca said as she opened the hatch.

Beth didn't object. He was her flight leader, after all, and he had every right to accompany her. Truth be told, she felt a little better with him coming. Beth hadn't done anything wrong, but not knowing what she was stepping into was not a terribly comforting feeling.

"You have no idea what this is about?" the lieutenant asked as they made their way to the center of the ship and CIC.

"Not a clue."

The *Bobolink* was a small ship, and they arrived at the hatch to the CIC within two minutes. Several sailors and Chipshot were milling about the passage outside the hatch, muttering amongst themselves.

"What are you two doing here?" Chipshot asked.

"She got called up," Salamanca said, tilting his head at Beth.

"What for?" Chipshot asked the other lieutenant.

Since the altercation in berthing two weeks ago, Chipshot no longer made fun of Beth and gave her a slight berth, and while he asked Lieutenant (JG) Salamanca the question, his eyes were locked on her.

"We don't know," Salamanca said.

One of the sailors, a chief, leaned in for a retinal scan, and the hatch opened. The three pilots started to enter when the chief said, "Only her."

The two officers exchanged glances with each other, but they didn't try and bluster their way inside.

Beth knew what a CIC was, but she'd never actually been inside of one. The *Bobolink's* CIC couldn't rival one on a bigger ship like the *Victory*, but it was pretty impressive none-the-less. This was both the brains and heartbeat of the ship. Beth didn't know what most of the stations did, and she didn't have time to try and figure it out. She gave it a single sweep, before focusing her attention on the ship's CO, the only other person inside the space.

Lieutenant Commander Tilok Hastert-Oona was young and looked younger. Beth had met him before, of course, but never alone like this. Close up, she realized that he didn't look quite as young as she'd previously thought. The weight of command had created tiny wrinkles at the corners of his eyes, and she could see just a hint of grey along his sideburns. Beth was a year older than the captain, and she wondered for a moment if she was also beginning to show the signs of age.

The CO's eyes, however, were bright and clear, and he said, "Thank you for coming, NSP2 Dalisay."

As if I had a choice.

"There's Class Zulu message for you," he said, pointing to the corner of the CIC.

Class Zulu?

Now Beth realized why the CIC crew had been evicted from their space and why the two lieutenants had not been allowed inside. A Class Zulu was a "for your eyes only" message from very high levels.

The question was why Beth would ever be on the receiving end of one. Her mind raced, but she couldn't come up with any logical explanation.

"For me?" she said before realizing how stupid that had to sound. He'd just said it was for her.

"Yep. For you."

The CO led a stunned Beth to the comms console. He didn't bother to sit, but bent and stuck his head under the hood. Beth couldn't hear what he said, but he slipped back out and motioned for her to sit.

"The Chief of Naval Operations is on the other side," he said before slipping the hood down over her head.

The Chief of Naval Operations herself? What in God's name is going on?

As soon as her head cleared the edge of the hood, she was in a windowless office, Admiral Canh sitting at the head of a table, Command Master Chief of the Navy Rains at her side, and two other admirals on either side of them. A silver-skinned GT sat next to the left-hand admiral, her somber business suit screaming high-level government-type.

The tech for the call was amazing. It was as if she was sitting across from the admiral, with none of the static or breaks that were always evident in commercial comms. She turned around, and as she half-expected, she had 360-degree coverage.

The CNO asked, "Are we secure, Master Chief?" Beth didn't see who he was speaking to and didn't hear the response, but it must have been positive because the CNO turned to look Beth in the eyes and said, "Let's get this show on the road.

"You're wondering what this is about," the CNO said as Beth nodded in agreement. "There's been a breakthrough with the situation on New Bristol, one that could have significant ramifications to the war effort. Unfortunately, we only received part of the information. With the planet-wide blackout still in place, this information was shot into space in a comms drone, and we received only a partial dump before it was destroyed. What we did receive was enough that we are placing this at the highest priority."

What in God's name has this to do with me?

"The handshake heading confirmed the subject's location, and the decision was made to extract the subject for a thorough debrief."

Beth kept her face passive, still wondering why the CNO herself was telling her this. She had a Top-Secret Bravo clearance, as had all the Stingers, but whatever this "subject" knew had to be way past Bravo.

"As you can imagine, this presents a problem. The crystals have a blanket over each of the captured planets. We can't just waltz in and pick him up. And that's where you come in."

Beth stared at the CNO for a moment, her mind not really making any sense from what the admiral was saying. She understood each word, of course, but together, they might as well have been some long-forgotten language.

"Ma'am?" she blurted out.

The CNO gave a grim smile, then continued, "You are being tasked with retrieving the subject." She saw the confusion on Beth's face, and she added, "We need something small, something stealthy, and something fast to get in and out with the subject and his samples. Something with enough power for a new scrambler as well. In other words, a Wasp."

"But ma'am, a Wasp is a single-seat fighter. There's no room for passengers."

"You did it once before, off SG-9222, with Chief Warrant Officer Nicolescu."

"That was an emergency, ma'am."

"And you don't think this is?" the CNO snapped.

Chastised, Beth shut up. None of this made sense to her, but then again, it wasn't often that what the top brass did made sense to her. Why should this be any different?

"Your Wasp will be stripped of its weapons . . ."

That caught Beth's attention. She was evidently going to have to land on an enemy-held planet, but she would be weaponless. She wasn't liking this at all.

". . . with the space the P-13 occupied acting as a cargo bay. We're not sure how much or large the samples the subject has, but the space will have to do."

"Ma'am, I'm not trying to be contrary, but have you considered a Wyvern? It's a two-seater."

The Marine atmospheric ground support plane was designed with a pilot and bombardier, and it could carry a heavy load of old-fashioned bombs and missiles. It wasn't nearly as capable as a Wasp in space, but it could get from point A to point B.

It looked like the CNO was going to bite her head off again, but she caught herself and said, "We did consider that. However, the consensus was that we can't make it stealthy enough, and it just doesn't have the git-up-and-go to outrun the crystals to safety. No, the Wasp gives us the best percentage of success."

"What's that percentage," Beth blurted, immediately regretting doing so.

The CNO's eyes narrowed, but she nodded and said, "Best case scenario? Twenty-nine percent."

Beth nodded back. At least it wasn't an automatic suicide mission, not that she'd have any say in the matter if it was. Orders were orders, and she was living on borrowed time as it was.

"I'm going to turn you over to Admiral Henderson for the details of your mission. Do you have any questions for me before I leave?"

Vice Admiral Mikey Henderson was the Vice-Chief for Operations, and it blew her mind that he'd be giving her operation brief. But she did have some questions that she wanted to ask the CNO.

"Can I ask who I'm picking up?"

"No, you cannot."

That might make it hard to find the guy.

"You'll be told with a milestone-release if you manage to reach the planet's surface."

"Very well. Can I at least ask what the information is that's so vital?"

"No, you may not." This time, she didn't add anything else.

Beth could see that she was going to go in blind. Hopefully, the vice admiral would give her a little more.

Beth was about to say she had nothing else, but she did, and it was bothering her.

"Why me? I mean, of all the pilots in the Navy, why me? I'm just an NSP2. Surely there are more experienced pilots."

The admiral gazed at her with a clarity as if they were in the same room, not separated by light-years. Beth could see the woman contemplate how much she could tell her.

Finally, she said, "You were not a unanimous choice, Dalisay. You are a known quantity, which brought you to the attention of the Directorate."

The Directorate is in on this? Beth wondered, glancing at the GT who'd been sitting quietly.

"That worked against you, to be blunt, right Mizee Tuominen?"

A Tuominen? A relative of the commander?

"True, Admiral," the GT said before turning toward Beth and adding, "Your value to the Directorate is already significant, and your exploits are well known to the populace. Most in the Directorate would rather your continued existence."

So, you don't want me to get my ass killed.

"The Directorate wants me in one piece. So, again, why me, then?" she asked, realizing that she was getting pretty cocky for an NSP2 speaking to the head of the entire Navy.

"Simple physics, Dalisay."

"Ma'am?"

"You're the smallest Wasp pilot in the Navy. The subject is not particularly small. You give us the most room in the fighter's cockpit to get him out."

Beth stared at the CNO for a moment, then burst out laughing. As a commercial scout pilot, a diminutive size was prized. In the Navy, the Wasps' powerful FC engines made a pilot's mass relatively meaningless, and in a world built for larger humans, her size could be somewhat limiting, something to overcome.

Now, she'd come the full circle. She was not being sent on a dangerous mission because of her piloting skills, but rather because of her size, the one thing she couldn't control.

The CNO looked at her as if she'd lost her mind. It took her a moment to gain control of herself. She wiped her eyes, then said, "So be it, ma'am. I'm your woman."

The CNO hesitated as if ready to change her mind, but she finally stood up and said, "I don't need to tell you how important this mission is. I've got full confidence in your abilities, so I won't wish you good luck. I merely charge you to perform to the utmost of those abilities, as I'm sure you will.

"And I'll remind you that this is Top Secret Kilo, and all of this stays with you. You won't tell your wingmates, your commander, or anyone what you are about to do. The commander of the *Bobolink* only knows enough to get you to where you need to be.

"And now, Admiral Henderson will give you your brief."

The CNO stood, and followed by the Command Master Chief of the Navy, the second admiral, and the civilians marched out of the room. The GT paused for a second and stared at Beth, but she didn't say anything.

Once the four had left the far-off conference room, the vice admiral pulled out a briefing control and said, "You are to commit this to memory. Nothing is to be recorded. The details you need will be on milestone-released message capsules, but for now, I'll be giving you an overview of the mission.

"The *Bobolink* will initially transport you and your Wasp to the *FS Calgary* for refitting . . ."

Beth was still in a daze. The mission seemed impossible, but impossible was the Navy's forte.

She turned to the vice admiral and listened intently. She may not get the next set of details until each milestone was reached, a process she'd seen on thriller vids, but never in real life. But if she hoped to get through this mission successfully, she needed every bit of info the vice admiral was going to give her.

FS CALGARY

Chapter 11

"She doesn't look that much different," Beth said, making her inspection.

"Not much was done with her hull," Lieutenant Commander Markel said, wiping his hands on his stained tanned overalls. "Most of the important upgrades were on the interior."

The lieutenant commander was dual-hatted as the *Calgary's* XO and engineering officer. With only 37 crew aboard the massive ship, most of the crew filled more than one position.

It had taken a full day after receiving the orders for the *Bobolink* and the *Calgary* to link up, a full day of direct and indirect queries on her mission. Beth never spilled, even to Mercy, who seemed rather put out. When Beth had returned to berthing and told the others that her mission was classified, Mercy had never considered that meant to her as well.

It had been a relief to finally leave her pouting friend and fly the *Tala* over to the big ship—although that had its own drama. Josh had begged to transfer to the *Calgary*, almost apoplectic that others would be working on his baby. Beth had tried to reason with him, telling him she would be returning to the *Bobolink* and he'd be stranded, but that hadn't done much good. He'd made her promise to keep a detailed list of everything the techs on the *Calgary* did to her so he could undo them at his first opportunity.

"That's not to say that we didn't do anything. Come take a look," the lieutenant commander said, flopping down on his back and pulling himself under the fighter. Beth hesitated for a moment. The *Calgary* was generally and surprisingly spotless, but not the specific area around the *Tala* where five techs had been working non-stop for the last 12 hours.

Hell, what am I worried about? Just a little dirt.

She got down and slid up alongside him.

"This is your P-13 housing. We removed the cyclotron, power converter, and lens."

For good reason, Beth was a little wary about hadron cannons now, and part of her approved the removal, but she would miss having the weapon with her. She'd never made a kill with hers, having splashed crystals with torpedoes and her rail gun, but that didn't mean the weapon was useless.

"Now, here," the lieutenant commander continued, pointing to a recessed latch, "is your access. Pull it out ninety degrees from here, rotate it like this, then flip it up."

The housing swung both out and open on a hinged edge, revealing a surprising amount of room, more than Beth would have guessed would be under a Wasp.

"When you want to close it, just reverse the actions," he said, demonstrating.

Beth reached up and touched the seam. She could feel a slight ridge, which wouldn't be a problem in the vacuum of space, and she hoped it wasn't disruptive enough to cause a problem in New Bristol's atmosphere.

"Can I put a person in there?" she asked.

"Can you? Sure!" he said.

Maybe I can stick my guest—

"If you don't mind him dying on you. There's no life support in there," he said with a laugh.

Har, har, sir. Very funny.

He shot himself backward with the skill of someone who'd done it a million times. Beth, half his size, had to inchworm herself back.

"We've taken out the rail gun and torpedo tubes. You might be able to stick some cargo in there as well, but you've got a limited diameter. I guess it depends on the size of the cargo . . ." he said, trailing the sentence off.

Beth didn't take the bait. The lieutenant commander didn't know her mission, but he was certainly curious. His whole team was curious. Beth had been isolated from the rest of the crew, even the CO, but she'd been watching the team work on her *Tala* the entire time.

"Tell her about the X-1000," AT2 Wu said, her voice almost breaking with excitement.

"I'm getting to that," he said. "This is sweet, and if it does what they say it will . . ."

He pointed to a tiny bulb that now protruded from the *Tala's* nose. This was the new cloaking device, the one designed specifically from the samples of crystal ship debris that had been collected. Maybe from the ship she and Mercy had captured, for all she knew.

The current cloaking and jamming had been somewhat effective against the crystals—at least, the humans seemed to detect the crystals farther out than the crystals detected them. But they were not 100% effective. In the Portland system, the Wasps had been picked up half a system away, which was farther than the crystals had previously demonstrated the ability. For every human advancement, the crystals seemed to match them.

This new system was supposed to be far more effective. It was unstable and a power hog, which was one of the reasons a Marine Wyvern couldn't be used for the mission, and it had never been field tested against human ships, much less against the crystals.

Other than that, what can go wrong? R&D would never lead me astray, right?

The lieutenant commander led her to the stern of the *Tala* where there was a matching bulb. Along with what looked to be some new standard wiring and a small control box that were installed inside, that was the totality of the new system. It sure didn't look like much to her.

The lieutenant commander was happily going over some specs, and from the expressions on the four enlisted techs' faces, they were eagerly following him. Beth smiled, but her thoughts were drifting. What was important to her was that when she turned it on, she became invisible. How it worked didn't matter, only that it did work. The X-91A system had just been installed, and it had been an upgrade. If this one was another advance forward, then all the better.

The *Tala* had lost her teeth, but now she had a cloak. Other than that, she should be the same *Tala* that had taken Beth into combat, and more importantly, back home each time.

Lieutenant Commander Markel finally ran out of things to say, Beth realized as he stood there looking at her expectantly.

"I think you did a fine job, sir. All of you," she added, sweeping an arm to include the others. "I'm sure the *Tala* will now help me accomplish my mission."

All five of them beamed at her.

"I'll be taking off in seven hours, so if you can bring me a cot and a meal, you can secure this space until then."

Second class petty officers didn't normally give orders to lieutenant commanders, and she hoped she didn't sound like she was doing that. The engineering officer/XO didn't blink, however, delegating the tasks to the others. Within five minutes, Beth was alone, locked inside the space with a cot and a surprisingly tasty meal of chili mac, fresh salad, and a chocolate cake of some sort. And a Coke, may God be praised.

She finished her meal and lay down on the cot. The *Tala* looked much the same, even if she was defanged. Hopefully, the upgrades would be enough to get her onto the planet and off with her passenger and his samples in one piece.

Beth checked the time as she closed her eyes and tried to get some sleep. She'd be taking off in six hours, thirty-one minutes. She'd find out soon enough.

NEW BRISTOL

Chapter 12

Beth was hurtling toward a gate that didn't exist.

That wasn't quite accurate. If the unknown scout had placed the mini-gate correctly, it did exist—it just wasn't powered up at the moment.

She kept her eyes locked on the display, but there was nothing. The mini-gate massed less than 30kg, and at full extension, created a nine-meter-by-nine-meter gate, roughly twice as wide as Beth and the *Tala* needed to pass through it. It was tiny in comparison to other gates, and far more problematic. Hit the gate off-center, and the right half of Beth would proceed to the New Bristol system while the left continued on her present course out in the middle of nowhere.

That gave Beth pause. She was used to shooting gates that could encompass battlecruisers or passenger liners. Not even being able to pick up the gate with her sensors made her nervous.

Of course, if the gate wasn't there, no harm, no foul, except to the mission. She'd have to return to the *Bobolink* without making it to the planet and wait for another attempt. It was that other possibility, the one where she was split in half that worried her.

No one was quite sure how the crystals had managed to locate and mine some of the gates, and the powers-that-be were trying to minimize the chance that this single, undersized and underpowered mini-gate would be detected. It would power up for five seconds, then shut down, hopefully too short a time for the crystals to notice.

On the way out, if they got that far, the *Tala* would shoot one of the two commercial or the single military gate into the system. Evidently, the planners were fine with her risking an unproven process to get there, but that would be different with her package aboard. They'd leave the system the tried and true way.

All of that would be meaningless if Beth didn't get into the system. She checked her count-down. Two more minutes and still nothing.

Beth pulled up the abort. It could be voice or touch-activated—Beth was going to do both. The red button was bright on her screen, and she placed the palm of her hand on the edge of the display, forefinger poised to push it.

If there was one thing Beth hated about flying, it was not being in control. Her old commercial Hummingbird had a very primitive AI, and very little of it was automated. Her Wasp was a multitude of generations more advanced, and the *Tala* could fly itself if need be. Like most fighter pilots, however, Beth liked to be in control. That wasn't going to work this time, and it was killing her. The timing and gate were just too tight to risk manual flying.

Her timer reached a minute, and still there was no sign of the gate. A 30 kg space rock had more than enough mass to be detected at this distance. The gate would have some stealthiness incorporated into it, but still . . .

Beth pulled out her silver cross, kissed it, then held it tightly in her right hand as the timer clicked down, her left finger twitching over the abort.

O most gracious Virgin Mary,

that never was it known that anyone who fled to your protection,
implored your help, or sought your intercession,
was left unaided.

Ten . . . nine . . . eight . . .
Oh, God! Where's the gate?
Seven . . . six . . . five . . . four . . .
That's it, she thought, her mouth opening to shout "Abort," her finger starting to drop when there was a flash on her display that froze her in place.

Two seconds later, she shot the gate and entered the New Bristol system.

****

Twenty-nine long hours later, Beth was approaching her entry angle. The transit from the gate, which had disappeared two seconds after she'd shot it, to New Bristol itself had been uneventful. There was plenty of traffic around the planet and what looked to be patrols out in the system at large, but none seemed to notice one small, unarmed Wasp. Maybe this time, the R&D folks with their X-1000 were on to something.

The speed limitations might not make the cloaking that practical for the entire fleet of Navy fighters. The gate and entry angle had been calculated to coast the *Tala* to her entry point to the atmosphere, her FC engine alight, but without propulsion, and her rate of speed entering the gate was far below a Wasp's capabilities. All the better to remain unseen.

That probably wasn't going to work on the outbound. Beth had to be ready to put the pedal to the metal and get to any of the three system gates she could. Those crystal patrols out there might try and have a say in that.

The *Tala* hadn't been completely quiescent during the transit, however. She had to slow down for entry, using passive and active measures. The passive relied on high-level physics that still were far beyond Beth's comprehension, but the active consisted of tiny, intermittent bursts of convention propulsion that were hopefully cloaked from observation.

Beth took over control of the *Tala*, running a quick check on the fighter. The course to the designated rendezvous was set, and all she'd have to do is course-correct on the way down. A Wasp was a hell of a space fighter, and it was pretty good in an atmosphere, too. It wasn't particularly aerodynamic, however, relying on brute power and thousands of micro-adjustments in her fuselage's skin to keep her flying true. Hopefully, Beth wouldn't have to make many control inputs, keeping her power emanations to a minimum until she was on the planet.

The bigger question was if her package—she still didn't know his name—would be at the location. The initial info packet had been time and location-stamped, but that was no guarantee that the package was still there, or if he'd even been there in the first place. Beth had no idea what to do if he wasn't there. Hopefully, her next milestone-release would tell her what was next if it came to that.

Truth be told, Beth was more than a little frustrated with the piecemeal information. She was off the ship and fully into the mission. Couldn't they just tell her now?

The Marines had this thing called "commander's intent." That meant the commander told their subordinates what they actually wanted done, the end result. They'd also issue a plan on how to accomplish that, but their subordinates could deviate from that plan as the mission progressed in order to best achieve the commander's intent.

Beth wasn't a Marine—thank the Lord—but the Navy could learn something from them. If Beth knew more of what was expected of her, she could adjust as needed to make sure she accomplished the mission.

As she approached the planet's atmosphere, her display showed her entry window. She was right on course, which was pretty remarkable for having been aligned before shooting the gate.

The *Tala* slipped into her approach. This was the tricky part of the mission.

No, just one of many tricky parts, she corrected herself.

Despite the new high-speed, low-drag cloaking, the *Tala's* mere physical presence would make disturbances in the atmosphere that could be observed. The hope was that if the crystals were watching, the *Tala* would look like a meteor.

Beth could feel the bite of the atmosphere, and she could see the glow of super-heated plasma envelope her fighter. With "super-slippery" skin, the friction was not as high as with ancient re-entry capsules, but physics could not be ignored. It was nigh on impossible to remain completely invisible.

Entering the atmosphere was one of her milestones, and a single chime alerted her to the next datadump.

"Your package is Doctor Lex Moran. Doctor Moran is a materials engineer with the Department of Resources, Mines and Minerals Division."

An official ID image appeared on her display of a mid-thirties, non-descript man staring blankly at the cam. He didn't look like much, just a forgettable face in a sea of humanity. Another image appeared, a snapshot of the same man, this time in full cosplay as a Portier Knight. The outfit was pretty remarkable, and unlike in his ID, the man looked alive and excited. This was obviously someone who took his time to get the details correct and who enjoyed what he was doing.

"Doctor Moran's message was clocked at Golf-tango-one-eight-three-six-two, Delta-Yankee-three-eight-eight-one-one."

Beth had already known that he'd be in the GT-DY grid, but not where within it. She pulled up the coordinates and area description. The spot was 42 klicks from Lockleaze, a mid-sized city along the Avon River in the midst of the second largest mining area on the planet. The river ran through a broad, thousand-kilometer-long valley, emptying into the Miller Sea at Avonmouth, some 300 klicks downriver. The area was forests, farms, and mines. Nothing on the ground near him should pose much of a problem.

The coordinates narrowed down the location to a single, 10-by-10-meter square, but there was no assurance that this Dr. Moran would be there. Hopefully, he'd at least be nearby.

There was only one way to find out. Beth edged the *Tala* into the cone. She might be at the controls, but her route in had been determined. Keeping to that flight path was a little tricky, though. A Wasp was kind of a brick as an aerodynamic body, and with the *Tala* powered down to 10% to reduce her signature, she was constantly adjusting to keep her on her glide path.

At about 60 kilometers, the *Tala* entered the stratosphere, ten klicks higher than Earth Standard. The ride smoothed out, and the planet spread out below her. Fully terraformed 86 years ago, forests, plains, and oceans stretched out below puffy clouds. A snow-capped range ran north and south on this continent, which wasn't her destination. It was beautiful, though. It was hard to believe that the planet was enthralled by the crystals, the population in peril.

As a reminder, there was a flash from a far-off booster, almost out of sight and where it was already night, as an ore carrier shot for orbit. The humans on the planet used a hybrid rail/booster system, and from initial observations, that system was still in use. The crystals were evidently more than willing to appropriate human systems.

In a conventional approach, Beth would take the *Tala* around the planet for a few orbits. But she was supposed to simulate a meteorite falling to the surface, so she had a direct shot in.

At least I'm falling like a rock.

If she hit at this speed, she'd splatter across the landscape. Beth would have to rely on a G-crushing flare to land safely.

The *Tala* streaked across the sky, over a brilliantly blue ocean, and finally went feet dry over the second continent, her target. Her approach was low, the thinner air and her low speed dropping her quicker than she'd expected. She goosed the engines a hair to gain a little altitude. She entered the planet's troposphere 560 klicks from her target.

This continent was not as rugged as the other. She crossed the first of the two ranges that made up the valley. No snow on these. Forests covered the rounded peaks.

She flashed by one mountain that looked to have been excavated to the ground, a dark stain against the green. Mining is what made New Bristol so valuable . . . and evidently made it a target for the crystals.

Beth wondered if the crystals were at this particular mine. There were huge excavators, looking like small yellow dots from her altitude, but she couldn't tell if they were even working, much less if they were being run by crystals.

Beth passed Broomhill at 9,000 meters. She was drifting low again, so she gave her engines another little boost.

That's more like it. Another four minutes to go, she thought, hoping that she wouldn't have to use her engines again until she came in for her landing.

Each time she used her engine, she kept expecting her alarms to go off, that she'd been spotted, but they remained mercifully quiet. She passed the vast Wimmerman mine complex off to the right, right on course and getting closer to her destination. It looked like she might actually land without being spotted. For the first time since she entered the system, she allowed herself to relax ever-so-slightly as she prepared for landing.

The gods of war were a capricious lot, and as if to punish her for assuming she was clear, a finger of fire reached out for the *Tala*. Acting on instinct, Beth took over, banking hard to the left. The rounds—they had to be kinetic rounds—whizzed past her canopy as she dove.

Her heart pounding, Beth tried to take the *Tala* down to the ground, hoping to use the rolling terrain as cover from whatever was firing at her. It didn't quite work. She was already closing the distance to the weapon, and diving didn't give her any separation. Another string of fire shot up from the ground, and at least one round connected with a loud clank.

Immediately, the *Tala* started bucking violently, throwing Beth hard against her harness. Her altitude plummeted, the ground rushing up to smash her.

She risked a glance out of her canopy. There was a hole in her fuselage where there shouldn't be, just forward of the engine compartment and just centimeters aft of the cockpit. From the way the *Tala* was fighting her, the round had probably taken out her starboard control surface interface. The *Tala's* AI knew the Wasp was in trouble, tried to correct, and when that didn't work, the feedback sent it into an ever-increasing spiral that would tear the ship apart. As she watched, more of her fuselage peeled back.

There was only one thing to do. Just as during her first encounter with a crystal, she killed the AI. She had to land the *Tala* by seat-of-the-pants flying. The problem was that still at over 2,000 KPH, she was screaming in smoking hot.

Her geodisplay had her 167 klicks from her target—there was no way her Wasp was going to stay aloft that far. Beth forced that from her mind and tried to concentrate on simply surviving. In a planetary air force flying an atmospheric plane, she'd punch out. That wasn't an option for her. Wasps were never made with ejection seats.

Beneath her, less than 1,000 meters, green forest whipped by. Any attempt to land among the trees at this speed would be deadly. She had to slow down, yet remain in control of *Tala* while it tried to fight her.

She needed better control. Beth flipped up the motile interface, slid her right hand in, and grabbed the "baseball," the slick "skin" enfolding her. The commands transmitted this way were finer, more detailed than the main controls used in space.

Here goes nothing!

Before she could second guess herself, she flipped the *Tala* in a twisting barrel roll, exiting the maneuver with the fighter's underside facing the direction of flight. It was like hitting a brick wall, and the *Tala's* compensators, which were never that effective under a planet's gravitational pull, could not alleviate all of the negative Gs. Beth felt like she'd been punched in the stomach.

Her ground speed dropped like a rock . . . as did the *Tala* herself. Her speed was cut by two thirds—not enough, but she couldn't afford to hit the ground tail down, nose up like that. She swung the nose down . . . and the *Tala* tried to roll again. The starboard control surfaces were going haywire. Her input was not making it through.

Acting instinctively, Beth activated the 3, 5, and 7 starboard thrust vectors with her left hand. The vectors were designed to increase maneuverability in space and were not intended for atmospheric flying. Beth didn't give a shit about that. She needed something, and that was all she had.

The *Tala* stopped the roll, then started to roll the other way. Beth cut back the power on the thrust vectors, and more by feel than anything else, edged the *Tala* into a steady flight.

Two hundred meters above the tops of the trees, she still had to slow down. She gave thrust vector #1 a goose, and the *Tala's* nose dipped, the body yawed. She shut off #1, and with a delicate touch, brought her to a relatively steady aspect again. A hundred meters lower, however. The odd tall trees here and there looked close enough to hit as she shot by.

She crossed herself with her left hand, then muttered, "Come on Floribeth. You can do it. Just figure it out."

Using tiny movements, she raised the nose five degrees. Not much, but a Wasp was not very aerodynamic, and it was enough. Her ground speed started to drop again.

At 150 kph, the *Tala* started to shake more violently, and she edged closer to the ground. Without full control of the starboard side of the fighter, Beth needed to remain in forward flight mode—she couldn't revert to V-STOL mode and set the Wasp down on any cleared area of ground. She didn't remember, however, how slow she could fly in this aspect and remain airborne, and she started to query her AI before she remembered she'd killed it.

Beth could make out more of the ground. What looked like dense forest before was now shown to have some open spaces, even a few fields. She knew she was running out of time. The Avon River was only a few klicks to her left, but the *Tala* would sink like a rock if she tried to land there. If she could even make the turn to reach it, that was. She had to put down on one of the open spaces, and soon.

That decision was made for her. There was a loud bang from the engine compartment, and the fighter started to yaw again. Just ahead, a field of some kind of grain stretched out.

"Mother Mary help me," Beth said as she dipped the nose, clipped a tree, and crashed teeth-jarringly hard on the ground. The *Tala* bounced back up, then pranged the ground again. Immediately, she cut the main propulsion and poured power to the bow thrusters, but all that did was spin the fighter around.

There was nothing she could do now but ride it out. She closed her eyes as the *Tala* bounced across the field, spinning like a top, expecting to slam into the trees at any moment.

And then, to her immense surprise, the *Tala* came to a lurching stop. She opened one eye. All she could see was green. Opening the other didn't change that.

For a moment, all she could think of was the *Tala* catching fire, like crashed spacecraft did in the holovids. She popped her harness, then the canopy, which only partially opened. She kicked at it wildly, widening the opening, then slithered out, fighting branches until she tumbled to the ground, landing hard on her side.

Beth struggled to sit up, breathing heavily from the adrenaline, her heart pounding. She drew her Navy issue Samsung M-20 from her thigh holster and stood up half-expecting crystal soldiers to come rushing up to her.

There were no crystals. There were trees, twenty feet tall, all around her, except for those that had been smashed by the *Tala* on the way in. Other than the hole in the fuselage just aft of the cockpit, the fighter looking mostly intact. She'd been afraid of the forest, but evidently, the *Tala* was built strong enough to survive smashing through trees of this size.

Beth turned to look down the path she'd cut out of the forest. A hundred meters away, the trees ended, and the path had been cut out of the grain in the adjacent field.

There may not be any crystals there at the moment, but they had to know that they'd shot her down and where. They'd be coming, and the smashed path through the grain and trees were a pretty good arrow pointing right at the *Tala* and her.

Beth had somehow survived getting down to the planet's surface. The question now was if she could survive what was coming next.

Chapter 13

During survival training at flight school, the instructors said that the best way to be found by rescue teams was to remain near the downed fighter. However, they also said that a downed fighter would be a draw for the enemy. Beth hadn't paid much attention to the details. Not many Navy pilots had been in that situation over the last couple of hundred years. Marines, yes. Navy, no. She'd considered survival training legalized harassment at the time, concerned only with putting up with it until it was over, the check mark in her training record.

As she stood alongside the *Tala*, however, she wracked her brain for whatever she could dredge up from the classes. Stick with her fighter or get away from it?

Beth didn't expect rescue. This was an enemy-held planet, after all, and she'd had to sneak in—unsuccessfully, as it turned out. If someone was coming, it had to be the crystals.

Get as far away as possible it is, then. But first . . .

She scrambled back up to the cockpit, reached in, and released her survival pouch, pulling it out and sliding back to the ground. She didn't even fasten it around her waist yet, instead, taking off at a jog deeper into the forest. For all she knew, the *Tala* was about to be zapped from orbit, and she had to get out of danger.

She was huffing and puffing within two minutes. Pilots needed to be in shape, and Beth spent the mandatory minimum time in the gym, but that didn't include running through a warm forest in her flightsuit after being shot down. Adrenaline and emotional stress had depleted her energy reserves, and her lungs screamed for O2.

After covering a couple of hundred meters, Beth slowed, scanning the woods for crystals. Birds flitted from branch to branch, ignoring her. She vaguely remembered one of the instructors saying something about watching the wildlife for signs of the enemy, but would birds take notice of crystals? The FALs weren't organic, after all.

Beth stopped by the trunk of a tree and took a seat. She was still holding the survival kit in one hand, her handgun in the other. With one last look around, she holstered the M-20 and opened the kit.

> Distilled water in pouch, (500 ml)
> Purification straw (1)
> High-Calorie Survival Biscuit (12)
> Squeeze LED flashlight (1)
> Multi-tool (1)
> Button Compass (1)
> Geoloc (1)
> Monofilament Line (10 meters)
> Thermal Blanket (1)
> Universal Translator (1)
> Firestick (1)
> Synthsteel Wire (2 meters)
> Signal Mirror (1)
> Class B First Aid Packet (1)
> 2l Water Bag (1)
> Emergency Beacon (1)
> Plastisheet (2)
> Pen (1)

Beth had passed on trying the infamous survival biscuits while in training. Each one had 4750 calories somehow jammed into it. She unwrapped one of them and tentatively took a bite. To her surprise, it wasn't bad, and she realized she was hungry. She continued to nibble on it as she looked at the rest of her gear.

The New Bristol citizens all spoke standard, and she doubted that the translator would work with whatever the crystals used to communicate. The beacon was probably equally as useless—no one was coming to rescue her. She was tempted to chuck them, but the entire kit only massed 900 grams, with most of that being the 500 ml of water.

Now what, Floribeth?

She was in a pretty tough situation—on a crystal-held planet without a working fighter to get her off. She didn't know the situation and probably had a platoon or whatever the FALs used coming to get her. But she also had her mission. That hadn't changed. The question was how she was going to accomplish it.

Beth pulled out the geoloc, then her heart sunk to the bottom of her stomach. She hadn't copied her target coordinates from the *Tala*.

"Satan's nuts!" she almost shouted, borrowing Mercy's favorite curse for the first time ever.

She stood and looked back toward where the *Tala* had landed. For all she knew, the crystals had already arrived and were on her trail.

There's no getting around it, she told herself.

Slipping the geoloc into her cargo pocket and closing the survival kit, she attached the kit to her belt and drew her M-20 again. Before she could talk herself out of it, Beth started jogging back the way she'd come. Every step brought her closer to the *Tala* and possibly the enemy.

She drifted slightly off course—she was a pilot, not a grunt—but the smashed trees and the bright red of the fighter were hard to miss. Slowing down, she carefully approached, alert to anything out of the ordinary. That didn't last long. Anxious to get the coordinates and get the hell out of there, she broke into a sprint for the final 20 meters, clambered up the side of the *Tala*, and wormed her head and upper torso into the cockpit, her ass and legs hanging out.

Half in and half out, she accessed her nav display. Her target coordinates were still there, along with the *Tala's* current location. She wasn't close: the *Tala* had landed 82 km from where she was supposed to be.

She held her disappointment at bay for the moment, not wanting to be overwhelmed. She tapped the geoloc to the display . . . and nothing happened.

"Come on, you bastard!" she hissed, tapping it again. Nothing happened. There was no transfer, so she did what anyone else would have done. She powered down the geoloc, powered it back up, then tapped again. This time, a soft chime answered her actions. The data transferred. She took a quick look. She had her location and her target. It hadn't changed her situation, but now, she at least knew where she was and where she had to go.

She almost collapsed for a moment in relief, then kissed the geoloc when a snap, like a breaking branch, reached her. She froze. The twittering of the birds cut off.

Beth was in a very compromising position, ass and legs outside of the cockpit, head inside. If this was finally her time, she wasn't going to go like this. She slipped the geoloc into her arm pocket, then gripped her M-20.

Beth had fought a crystal before, and she knew her little handgun wasn't going to be very effective, but it was the only thing she had. She'd managed to kill that crystal by hitting its breathing apparatus, poisoning the thing with O2. She wasn't a good enough shot to count on doing that again.

Another branch snapped, then a third. They were getting close.

Her heart pounded as she started to worm herself back out of the cockpit, her feet reaching for purchase. Her only chance was to slide out quietly before they detected her, then run. She had no idea how fast a FAL could move over ground, but she figured she was about to find out.

Almost out of the cockpit, she held on to the edge, elbows bent and feet reaching for the ground. She was too short. Beth started to lower herself when her right hand slipped and she fell with a thud, her left leg buckling.

She caught motion in the corner of her eye, something coming out of the forest. Expecting to feel the net-thing that had caught Mercy on Toowoomba, Beth rolled as fast as she could, hoping to spoil the thing's aim, all while trying to bring her little M-20 to bear. Somehow, she rolled to a kneeling position, ready to fire . . . and froze.

Four humans in mismatched camouflage and carrying hunting rifles were staring at her in wonder.

Chapter 14

"I don't know," Horace Parmalee said, peering into the gap in the *Tala's* fuselage. "The engine shell ain't broke, thank Elyese. If she was done for, so would we. Can't no way replace an FC."

"Can you fix it, then?" Beth asked, looking over her shoulder down the path the *Tala* had cleared in the trees, wishing the man would hurry up.

Horace, Yeti Chen, Randy del Torro, and Whisper White had been almost as surprised to see Beth as she had been to see them. The four, part of a local unofficial militia, had rushed to the crash site thinking it was a crystal ship that had gone down, and they were hoping to scavenge anything that could help their cause, said cause being throwing the crystals off their planet. They'd been overjoyed to see a Navy pilot, assuming that she was the vanguard of the hoped-for human assault. Beth had put somewhat of a damper on their enthusiasm by telling them she was simply a scout, trying to gather intel.

Beth still didn't have a grasp of how they planned on freeing the planet on their own. From initial comments, she thought the four were part of a loosely organized small group of people who'd been lucky enough to be missed by the initial crystal assault. That wasn't important now, though. After Horace examined the *Tala*, wondering if he could patch her up, that became Beth's foremost priority . . . that and getting it done before the crystals inevitably arrived on the scene.

"That tube on the right, going into the engine—I don't know quite what it does, but I manage I can jury rig a patch. What do you think, Yeti? A Bryson?"

The young woman looked in again, then said, "Don't know the pressure on that thing. Maybe a KP-Four? The Bryson could blow."

"Yeah, you're probably right," Horace said after a moment's contemplation. "Better safe than sorry."

Beth was getting more anxious by the moment. The four had acknowledged that the crystals would come to investigate, but the two were calmly discussing what to do with the fighter as if this was a local hover repair shop.

"Now, this right here," he said, tapping something that Beth couldn't see, "this here's the problem. I'm guessing that it controls the flight surfaces for this half of the plane."

Beth perked up at this. She hadn't told him that she'd crashed because she'd lost her starboard controls. Maybe he did know something about "planes."

"The problem is that this is a government plane, and you know how behind the curve they are. The control is qubit, and we don't have no qubit processors to handle something like this."

Despite the situation, Beth almost bristled at the comment. A Wasp was the pinnacle of human technology, and he said it was behind the curve?

"Wimmerman—hell, *all* the mines—we use NML for this kind of computing power."

Beth knew what NML, Nanomagnetic Logic was. The Navy's big research computers were NML, as were some of the shipboard CIC computers, but not, as far as she knew, any of the smaller vessels' computers. There had to be a reason for that, but Beth didn't know enough about the science to defend the Navy's systems.

"Do we have a WU-1001?" Horace asked Yeti as if Beth was no longer standing half a meter behind him.

"Yeah, at the site."

"You ready to ask one them damned aliens if you can get access to the shop?" Horace said, rolling his eyes. "I meant at the transit depot."

"Maybe. They came through sometimes," Yeti said.

"I'm thinking, that if we can get one, me and you can gyver up a translating processor, you know, to put out a signal the control junction can understand."

"Won't be the same speed," Yeti said.

"No, shit. But if the pilot here takes it easy, I think a Yale synch, or maybe a Pearson-4901 . . . no, the five series . . ."

Beth was lost. She had no idea what the two were saying. She looked again down the path of downed trees, half-expecting to see the crystals while the two argued.

"Uh . . . I hate to ask again, but you said the FA—the crystals—would come to investigate?" she asked Whisper.

"Ayah. They will, but they're pretty slow to react here in the boonies. If you'd crashed your plane . . ."

Fighter, not "plane."

". . . closer to Lockleaze or one of the mines, they'd have already swarmed you." the older woman said. "Here, it might be a day before they send a carafe."

"Carafe?"

"Oh, sorry. Just one of our terms. Carafe. Like a crystal glass. They usually send six of them out at a time."

It didn't make much sense, but Beth let it go.

"Are you sure about that. I mean, with those two . . ." she trailed off, tilting her head at the two with their heads huddled around the hole in the *Tala*.

"Yeah, we have time, and if anyone's gonna get your plane back in the air, it's Horace. Him and Yeti."

"Him?" Beth asked, her tone making it obvious she had her doubts.

Horace was maybe in his mid-sixties, clad in a pair of blue sweats, a weird orange-and-brown-toned camouflage, and a battered red Suntori baseball cap. He might be a decent-enough mechanic, but despite what he said about the government, the Wasp was not some off-the-assembly-line hover.

"'Him' is Wimmerman's chief engineer, and Yeti's one of his doctoral candidates, come all the way from Liberty Station to study under him," Randy said.

"He's a chief engineer, and a Ph.D.?" Beth asked, her mouth dropping open.

With his demeanor and odd syntax, she was shocked . . . and more than a little ashamed. She'd always fought being summarily dismissed because of her size, and yet here she was dismissing Horace because of the way he spoke?

"He was out at the remote lab when the crystals hit us, thank God," Whisper said. "Too few of us missed the sweep."

Completely wrapped up with her mission and her deadlined Wasp, Beth had almost forgotten that the New Bristolians had suffered a deadly invasion.

"How many, you know, in the assault?" she asked quietly.

"We don't know. Ten, maybe twenty percent within an hour. Now? Most of the people are being held prisoner in the cities and mine sites," Whisper said.

"Biological shields," Randy added. "We can't do anything about it. "If we try, they'll kill our folks."

"And how many of you are there? Out here and armed."

The two exchanged glances, and Whisper gave the briefest of nods.

"With us? Twelve. But there's more out there. We've seen the signals," Randy said defensively.

Beth had to fight to hold back a frown. *Twelve? And they want to take back the planet? Laudable, but hardly practical.*

"I said, Petty Officer, that we might be able to get this plane back in the air," Horace was saying.

"Really? That's great!" Beth said, turning back to the two. "And she'll be spaceworthy?"

"To an extent. I'd not want to be pushing here. There'll be a time lag issue that won't stand up if you go into high-g dogfights with crystal fighter planes. But keep the stress down, and I'm reasonably sure your plane will fly again. If we have the right components," he qualified.

"Reasonably sure?" "Right components?" Well, that's better than nothing, I guess. Better than I stood twenty minutes ago.

"How long will it take you? I've still got my mission to complete."

"Well, we can't do it here, not the least because the crystals will eventually come and investigate. But we need a shop to get it done. So, unless you can fly it, even at low speed . . . ?"

Beth shook her head.

"Didn't think so. So, we haul it. Yeti here will go scrounge up what we need, then meet us there. If all goes well, five days, I'd say."

"Five days!" Beth said, feeling a bit of panic.

"Yeah, I think we can manage that," Horace said, obviously pleased with himself.

For Beth, five days was an eternity. She didn't know if her package would still be there, and each day delayed raised the probability that he'd abandon his position, thinking no one was coming.

"There's no way you can do it quicker?" she asked, turning toward Horace.

"Possibly, but we need the components," Horace said, frowning slightly. "If we had access to the main site, yes. But that's controlled by the crystals."

The four were looking at her, waiting for her response. If five days was the soonest they could repair the *Tala*, then it was what it was. It might work.

"And I can then fly it farther north after that?" she asked, working out a new timeline in her head.

"North? From here?" Whisper asked. "You'd get shot down again. You were lucky to get it this far, but the crystals have far more defenses set up to the north. Lockleaze is a fortress. No way you'd survive."

Then it doesn't matter if it's five days or five months, she thought as a feeling of helplessness sought to overcome her. *Fight it, Floribeth! Think of something.*

No solution magically popped into her mind. She wished she had comms back to the squadron to ask what to do.

Even with the *Tala* repaired, if Whisper was right, then she couldn't fly up to retrieve her package. That left one option that she could think of. If Mohammed won't go to the mountain, then the mountain has to come to Mohammed.

The four were looking at her, waiting for her to say something. She took a long moment, wondering how much she could tell them.

Screw it. I need their help.

"I'm not a scout. I'm here on a special mission to retrieve someone and get them off-planet."

All four looked at her in shock, mouths dropped open.

"You can do that??" Randy asked.

"Who is it," Horace demanded. "Who rates such a specific rescue?"

They edged closer to her, not looking happy, and Beth involuntarily took a half step back.

"I can't tell you. I'm sorry. But I can assure you that he's needed. What he has will be a huge boost to the war effort."

I hope. I just don't know for sure.

The four glared at her, then Whisper said, "So, why are you telling us this? What do you want from us?"

"Do you know where this is?" Beth asked, taking out her geoloc and turning on the small display.

"Yeah," Randy said after a quick glance. That's along Montoya Highway, between Lockleaze and Saint Aspin. I know the area. Is that where, you know . . .?"

"Yes. I am supposed to pick up my package. I mean, the person. If he's still there. I can't really wait, and if I can't fly to him, I need to get him here. Can you take me there?" she asked Randy.

"I guess I could, but I don't like breaking up our team."

"I'll go with you," Whisper said. "Horace, you and Yeti handle her plane. This is a Navy pilot, and if she says this will help the cause, then it's our duty to do what she says."

Whisper looked at the other three for a long, pregnant moment before Horace turned to Yeti and asked, "You think me and you can move this thing on our own?"

"I'd say so. We're near enough to the one-twenty-kilometer maintenance station that we can grab a mule and get back here. Two hours, tops. Load the plane up, go back down to the farm," she said, pointing down the path the *Tala* had cut, "and then up to the road. As long as a carafe doesn't come up the road, we should be home free."

"That's settled, then," Whisper said before turning to Beth and asking, "When do you want to leave?"

"Now's as good a time as any."

"Then let's move out. We've got a long, hard, walk in front of us."

Chapter 15

Beth stopped for a moment and wiped the sweat from her brow. Whisper hadn't been joking when she said they had a long haul in front of them. Eighty-two kilometers was nothing in a Wasp, a fraction of nothing. On foot, it was forever. Beth had never been so tired, so aching, in her life.

Whisper had given her a camo jacket, which she wore over her flightsuit. She'd need the suit when—she forced herself to use "when" in her thoughts, never "if—she took off with her package, and it didn't fold up nice to carry. So, she was hot and sticky.

Her flightsuit booties were designed for control in the cockpit, not for long marches. Her feet were on fire, each step torture. She wanted to stop and collapse against one of the innumerable tree trunks she passed, but she thought that if she sat, she'd never get up again.

"Are you OK?" Whisper asked, stepping up beside her.

Whisper was obviously tired, too, but the older woman was either not suffering as much as Beth was, or she was better at hiding her exhaustion. That shamed her. Beth was young and in the Navy. Whisper, as Beth found out as they trekked through the forest, was a 55-year old accountant. She'd missed the assault and roundup while traveling across the mountain range, returning from the coastal city of Exmouth where she'd visited her son and grandkids. She'd no idea what had happened, only that her livefeed had cut off while in the pass. Wondering if someone at Wimmerman's Lyston facility could fix it, she turned off the highway, only to be stopped by Randy and three others at a roadblock. Without that roadblock, Whisper would have been scooped up by the crystals.

"Yeah, I'm fine," she told Whisper, then pointed at her feet. "These things aren't really made for marching."

"Sorry my feet are so big," Whisper said.

"Sorry my feet are so small."

Whisper had an extra pair of jingos, the shock-cushioned athletic shoes, in her backpack, but Beth's feet were swimming in them when she tried them on. At least her flightsuit booties fit.

Randy, walking in front of them, stopped and held up a hand. He looked at Beth's geoloc, then up at the forest in front of them, then down at the geoloc again.

"I think we're going to have to go around here. I didn't realize that we were so close to Jin Ling's lanthanum mine."

That wasn't what Beth wanted to hear. They traveled about 60 clicks in two days and were only 20 from her target.

"How far will that send us?" she asked.

"About another ten klicks, I'm guessing. To be on the safe side."

Beth looked up at the planet's sun, almost straight overhead. She was hoping to reach their destination before dark, find her package, and be on the way back. If they detoured another ten klicks through the forest, there was no way they'd reach it until tomorrow.

"Is the detour imperative?" she asked.

"Imperative? Not really, I'd guess. But to be safe. The crystals are swarming the mine sites, and you never know what the buggers are doing there at any given time."

Beth weighed the options. She could go along with Randy and push off arriving until morning, giving her package one more opportunity to call it quits, or she could have them push on.

"Can I see my geoloc?"

Randy handed it over, and she studied it for a moment, trying to orient herself. She could see their present position, that of her target, and a route to it using minor roads and trails.

"Can you show me this mine?"

Randy pointed to an area just adjacent to the displayed route. "It runs from about here to here. I'm suggesting we parallel Route 33 down to Pander, then cut back along this road here. Uh . . . Torrent Road. That's lead us back to Route 15, and we can take that in."

Beth studied his route, but she didn't want to take it. An extra ten klicks were more than she wanted to tackle right now.

"How about we just get off this road and move into the woods farther."

"Road" was pretty generous for what was little more than a dirt trail. It made walking easier, but that was about it.

"It was pretty rough coming over the hills," Randy said. "Are you up for that?"

It had been rough going cross-country for several klicks. The forest looked pretty tame, but the undergrowth of brambles and brush had been difficult to pass through. For the life of her, Beth couldn't understand why the terraformers of so long ago bothered with putting thorn bushes in the new world.

"I'm up for it. Time is of an essence, so, let's go for it."

"OK, you're the boss," Randy said, taking back the geoloc.

He led them off the trail, deeper into the forest, then turned to parallel it. Beth could barely see the trail, but her geoloc should keep Randy on course.

Within five minutes, Beth was regretting her choice. The going was much more difficult than walking the trail, and she was sweating like a racehorse. She'd long downed her survival water, filled her water pouch twice in streams they' crossed, and emptied it. She needed to find another wa source soon, or she'd have to break down and ask Randy for a couple of swallows of his.

After another 30 minutes, she decided she had to ask him if she wanted to keep going. She stepped up, hand out to touch him on the shoulder when he dropped as if shot.

He twisted on the ground and motioned for Beth and Whisper to get down.

"What is it?" Beth asked, only to be hushed by him.

She was only a meter or so behind him, so she pulled out her M-20 and crept up alongside the man. He put a finger over his mouth, then pointed ahead. Beth tried to see what he was pointing at through the leaves, and she had to move over just a bit until she saw it.

A crystal was motionless in a small clearing ahead. Not really motionless. It wasn't moving over the ground, but it was tossing, if that was the word, a small rock, from one crystal tine, over its bulk, and catching it on another tine before tossing it back.

The crystal was about the same size, maybe 500 kg, like the one she'd killed on Toowoomba. Mostly silver and black, she picked up hints of blue and purple depending on the angle of the crystal facets. Like the other one, this one had the breathing apparatus attached to it.

Beth wondered what the heck it was doing. The rock it was tossing tinked with a musical tone each time it hit a tine. After a few tosses, Beth realized the tone was different each time the rock hit. There had to be a rhyme or reason for what it was doing. Juggling? Singing?

The thought that the crystal might be doing something as innocuous as that bothered Beth. She'd long thought of the crystals as mindless automatons, not really alive in the same way humans were. But the more she watched, the more it looked like this crystal was just lazing away the time—just like a human.

Whisper tapped her foot. She turned, and the woman was tilting her head to the right, mouthing, "Let's go."

Beth gave one more glance at the crystal, then slowly crept backward. They'd bypass it, and she'd tell Randy to offset even farther from the trail.

Whether it heard (if they even hear) her getting up or one of the others, Beth didn't know. One moment, there was the ting, ting, ting, of rock juggling, then a loud clang and a rush of motion. Beth whipped her M-20 around just in time to see the massive crystal rush her, clicking like crazy. She fired twice, both rounds ricocheting off. She didn't have a clear shot at the breathing apparatus.

Randy shoved her aside, then fired his Winchester-Simmons .380 at a range of ten meters. The heavy, high-velocity round shattered the right side of the creature, shards of crystal flashing in the sun. The clicking sped up almost to a single tone as the crystal shuddered to a stop, the remaining tines waving weakly, like a sea urchin in the bottom of the boat. A single white tine shot out, the same kind that had almost captured Mercy, but it fell short of the three humans. Randy stepped forward, aimed right into the center of the thing, and fired twice more.

The middle of the crystal shattered into a thousand pieces, and the clicking cut off. It was dead. Randy's hunting rifle had more than enough punch to drop the thing.

Beth holstered her little M-20, unable to break her eyes away from it. She'd fought crystals many times before. She'd killed more than her fair share. But this was only the second time she'd actually seen one. This made it all the more real, somehow.

Randy loaded three more rounds into his magazine, still looking at his kill until Whisper pulled him back by the shoulder.

"Come on. We've got to get out of here," she said, quietly but firmly.

It seemed to sink in. Randy shook his head like a drunk trying to sober up, then said, "Right. Let's go."

Beth didn't say a word as she followed him deeper into the forest.

Chapter 16

They didn't reach the target that day. After Randy killed the crystal, Whisper thought they'd be smart to push deeper off the track, and then more general enemy activity deflected them even farther. The crystals didn't seem to slow down at night, which shifted the advantage to them and increased the chances that the next time, it would be the crystals that spotted the humans first. So, the three hunkered down under the bluff of a small creek for the night.

Beth doled out three of her survival bars. Neither Whisper or Randy had expected to leave on a cross-country trek, and they'd eaten the last of their food during the day. They munched on the bars in silence, then Beth filled her water pouch from the creek, sterilized it, and shared that as well.

As with the night before, the two wanted to know what had happened since the crystals arrived. Beth did the best she could. The problem was that she'd been in the hospital for part of the time and caught up with her job and being on a ship under comms silence for most of the rest. She didn't have much to offer.

What she didn't tell them was what happened to Portland. She felt guilty for holding back, but she thought it was better not to stress them out.

"Well, we'd better get some sleep," Whisper said. "Randy, you take the first watch. I'll take the second. You can have the third," she told Beth.

Which was fine with her. Her body ached, and she needed to get some rest, even if that was sitting on the dirt, back up against the bluff walls.

It seemed like only a few minutes when Whisper woke her up. She warned Beth to listen for crystals who might be tracking them, the first time Beth had even considered that. Coupled with the normal sounds of nocturnal animals and branches rubbing against each other in the breeze, that kept her on a hair trigger, Randy's .380 laying across her lap. She gave an audible sigh of relief as dawn broke and she could wake the others.

After a quick breakfast of her Navy survival bars, the three slipped through the woods, Randy back on navigation and bending them around toward the destination. Beth got more and more nervous, hoping her package was there, but afraid that he wouldn't be.

Midmorning, with an overcast that had crept up while they walked, they finally reached their target, which was one of the old terraforming stations, long since abandoned. Most of the repurposable equipment had been removed, leaving the control center and the huge projector. The building was falling apart, courtesy of nature trying to reclaim the spot, and the projector canted to the side as if some of the supports had been scavenged.

Still, it was pretty impressive—not so much for what it was now, but for what it had been. New Bristol had been a live world, but nothing higher on the evolutionary chain than lichen-like analogs. Those still existed—or they had until the crystal invasion, at least—under a number of protected biodomes. The rest of the planet was a haven for humanity, thanks in part to a thousand such projectors which pumped out O_2, water vapor, and other gases for decades until the terra-engineers could come in and introduce the new ecosystem.

But she wasn't here to marvel at technology. She had to find her package. If he wasn't here, she didn't have a clue as how to proceed. Something about the projector was niggling at the back of her mind, but whatever it was, escaped her. She shook her head, and stepped up to the door to the control center, automatically raising her hand to knock, then laughing and pushing the door open.

There was nobody inside, just leaves and the strong smell of urine. Animal droppings of some sort were scattered across the floor.

"Doctor Moran?" she asked in a quavering voice, hoping for a response.

Nothing.

"Doctor Moran?" she said again, raising her voice.

Again, nothing.

"Is he here?" Whisper asked, stepping in and alongside her.

"If he is, he's not answering," Beth said, feeling frustrated, afraid that the last three days had been wasted.

"Doctor Moran!" Whisper shouted, as if she thought her voice could make a difference.

"Well, let's search the place," Beth said. "He could still be here."

"What about Randy? Him, too?"

"No, leave him there," Beth said after a moment's consideration.

She'd left Randy out by the road where he could watch with his Winchester-Simmons. Whisper's comments the night before about the crystals tracking them had stuck in her mind. She'd asked Whisper about it again in the morning, and the woman had confirmed that the crystals had done it before.

The two searched the entire control center, checking every room, every cupboard, every closet. There were a few signs of humanity, but no doctor. Frustration was giving way to despair. As long as Beth had a mission, she could put up with getting shot down, with hiking 82 klicks, possibly with crystals tailing them. Without a mission—and without Dr.

Moran, she had no mission—she didn't know what to do. She'd simply be stranded on a planet that could be destroyed at any moment.

And suddenly, she knew why the terraforming projector had been an itch in her mind.

"Has there been anything odd with the crystals?" she asked Whisper.

"Odd? Other than the fact that they're fucking made of crystal? Or that they took over my planet? No, not odd at all," Whisper said, sarcasm dripping from her voice.

"Yeah, of course. I mean, have they built something odd? Like the projector," Beth said, pointing at the ceiling and the projector on the roof.

"Like that? I haven't heard anything. Why?"

"Oh, nothing for sure."

But there was a reason for asking. No one knew yet how the crystals had destroyed Portland. It wasn't from a planet buster, nor did it seem to be from a ship at all. It had to be something on the planet, and the theoretical scientists, after analyzing the data, thought it might be a geometrically emplaced array of some sort.

Beth might never find Dr. Moran, but if Beth could find out how the planets were booby-trapped, then get off the planet far enough to report that back, then still had a purpose.

It was a case of trying to salvage a mission that she could accomplish.

Not that this one was over. There were still more places to look.

She pointed to the access ladder that led to the roof and said, "Shall we?"

The stairs were basic metal. Some of the bottom rails had been scavenged, but the steps were still solid . . . she hoped. After the first landing, the rails were still attached, which made it easier. Beth was afraid that the door onto the roof would be locked, but it swung halfway open at her push until it stuck. Whisper followed as she stepped through and out onto the roof.

Weather had not been kind to the black surface. It was warped and torn. Beth hoped that the underlying structure was sound, but she was going to keep herself to where the surface looked the least degraded.

This close to the edge, she looked down and spotted Randy at the entrance. She waved, but he was intent on what was potentially out there, not what she and Whisper were doing. Very professional of him and not bad for a facilities maintenance technician without military training.

"I keep forgetting how big those things are," Whisper said from beside her.

Beth turned to look up at the projector. It was big. Huge. It had to be to have been able to put out the millions of kilotons over the course of decades. Powered by exchangers sunk deep inside the planet's core, it had been designed to run non-stop with little or no maintenance. It seemed sad that it had been left to decay once its mission had been completed.

"Let's check it out," Beth said, leading a crooked path along what looked to be the best of the roof.

Her eyes were drawn to the projector above her as she approached, and she got within five meters before she caught sight of what looked to be a pile of rags on the roof, up against the base of the projector.

She stopped dead in her tracks, holding up an arm to stop Whisper as well. It wasn't a pile of rags but rather an emaciated man lying on the roof, one arm protectively around a container of some sort. She couldn't tell if he was alive or dead.

"Hello? Are you OK, sir?" she asked to no response from the man.

"Is that . . . ?" Whisper asked.

"I'm not sure," Beth said. "It could be."

She took a couple of steps forward, reached out a foot, and nudged the man's foot. One eye flashed open, a deep-hazel eye, almost green, and Beth realized this was her package.

"Doctor Moran, I presume?" she said, having planned her greeting when she first left on her mission.

The eye stared at her until slowly the other eye opened. Moran opened his mouth to speak, coughed, then licked his lips and tried again.

"Well, I see someone's a comedian. You don't look like Henry Stanley, but yes, I'm Doctor Moran."

Beth hadn't gotten beyond that greeting, so she stammered out, "NSP2 Floribeth Dalisay, Navy of Humankind. I'm here to take you back."

"About time. I've been here for a . . . hell, I don't know how long."

Beth knelt beside him and offered him her water pouch. He came to life, sucking down the water until a fit of coughing overcame him.

"I'm sorry about that. It took a while for us to get the rescue attempt planned, and there were problems."

"After what I sent back, this should have been the top priority," he said, struggling to sit up.

The water had given him a shot of energy, but he was still weak.

Beth gave him the benefit of the doubt, given his condition. No matter what he'd discovered, it was important. Her very presence attested to that. But he could be overestimating what the directorate was willing to do to get him and his information back.

He looked around the roof and frowned. "If you're taking me back, I don't see a ship here. What are we going to do? Walk?"

"No, I had to land somewhere else. We'll walk there."

"Walk? I'm not sure I'm up to that. Why do you think I chose this site? No crystals within kilometers and a clear enough area to land."

"I didn't land somewhere else on purpose. I was shot down," she said, starting to be just a little bit annoyed with the man. When his eyes opened wide, she added, "But the *Tala* is being repaired. It should work by the time we get there."

"It'd better be. This is vital," he said, his eyes drifting to Whisper.

"I know you. You're a Wimmerman bean counter."

"I am," Whisper said, her eyes narrowing. "But I don't know you."

"Lester Moran, DRMMD. Chief Materials Engineer."

Beth didn't understand the dynamics involved, but Whisper nodded. This Doctor Moran evidently carried some weight with the mining companies.

Beth pulled out her last survival bar and offered it to the man, who greedily grabbed it, then ate it with more gusto than the thing deserved.

"You're starving, sir. Why didn't you get off the roof and find some of the survivors? There're more than a few of us around," Whisper asked.

"I couldn't risk it. I couldn't leave this up here," he said, patting the case beside him, "and I couldn't take it with me in case the crystals caught me."

"Can I ask you what's in the case?" Beth asked.

"You don't know?"

"No. Your message was corrupted. We never found out."

"Well no wonder they sent only you," he muttered to himself before turning to Beth and Whisper and saying, "This, ladies, may be the key to what we need in this war."

He waited for a dramatic, drawn-out pause before saying, "What I have in here is a live baby crystal!"

Chapter 17

Beth stared at the case. They'd hauled it down the stairs into the control center, going slow as Moran could barely stand upright. One-by-one-by-a-half-meter, it didn't look like much. But if Moran was telling the truth, it could be the most valuable half-cubic meter in the galaxy.

A living crystal was the holy grail to the war effort, and right there, not two meters from her, there it was. A single green light indicated that it was still alive. If it switched to red, well, she didn't want to think of that.

Dr. Moran hadn't told them just how he'd acquired the baby. He'd simply assured them that as long as his case was powered up, the crystal was in a sort of hibernation, almost in a stasis state.

Beth wanted to see the thing. It wasn't that she didn't trust Moran, but it didn't make sense. How did he just happen to have it, and how did he have a case to hold it? She couldn't imagine a human acting in concert with the crystals, but she was suspicious.

"Yes, that's right," Moran was telling Whisper. "They're using our minerals to grow more things. Ships, weapons, baby crystals."

"Wait, you're telling me they grow each other *and* their ships? Grow?"

"Why not? They're made of the same materials. It's just a matter of manufacturing."

"But they're crystalline. Not metal," Whisper protested.

"And what is metal? At a microscopic level, it's already in crystal form. Furthermore, metal atoms characteristically shed electrons to form positive ions, and this property can be used to cause metals to form crystals."

"But babies *and* ships? Live and inanimate?"

Moran shrugged and asked, "What is life? I personally don't know, but I'm guessing the 'live,' as you call it, crystals use more lanthanum."

He looked over at Beth and asked, "Do you have another of those bars?"

"That was the last one, sir. We'll figure out something and get you fed," she told him.

"I haven't had anything to eat for the last couple of days," he said, turning back to Whisper. "What I wouldn't give for a Winston right now."

"Stop it! A double cheese with onion straws! My God, I've missed them!" Whisper said.

Beth didn't know what a Winston was, and she didn't care. She was still trying to process everything she'd heard over the last half hour. Some of what he was spouting bordered on the unbelievable, but there was just enough in there that she recognized so that what he could be saying was true.

Take the comment about lanthanum. Beth had studied up some after she'd killed the crystal on Toowoomba, and the remains had been collected and studied. The FAL had lanthanum in its body, and she'd read that the lanthanides could bind with more electronegative atoms, such as oxygen or fluorine. Or chlorine, which was what the crystals breathed.

It just seemed weird that the crystals were on the planet to mine titanium, iron, and lanthanum, then manufacturing baby crystals. Humans didn't collect carbon, after all, to make babies.

Her doubts didn't matter, however. She had her orders to bring the doctor and his "sample" back to human control. She'd do that and let smarter people than her work out what to do next.

She still wasn't sure how she was going to do that. Moran was weak, and she didn't think he was up for the long trek back. She had to get him food and build up his strength. The longer she waited, though, the greater the chance at discovery. It looked like they'd escaped the consequences of killing the crystal the day before, but she couldn't count on that kind of outcome forever.

Heck, the brass might try and invade, and then Moran and his baby crystal won't make it off the planet. Or me.

Beth decided that the first order of business was to send Randy off to find some food. He should know where was safe and where wasn't. Maybe tomorrow they could start back, but only traveling a few hours each day. Moran might be able to handle that after some chow in his belly and a good night's rest.

She stood up while the two went on about their favorite foods and walked to the entrance to signal Randy. To her surprise, Randy was already sprinting back. She stopped just outside the door, waiting for him.

He saw her and still at a full run, shouted, "We've got to go. The crystals are coming!"

Chapter 18

"You can't give up," Beth told Moran, one arm around his waist.

"Sorry, I'm just—"

"Don't be sorry. Just do it," Beth snapped, trying to use her best voice of command.

Moran nodded, then picked up the pace.

Beth didn't know where they were going, just that 1500 meters or so behind them, the crystals were on their trail. That meant the way forward was anywhere the crystals were not.

She was kicking herself for almost getting them all caught. If the crystals had reached them while they were in the control center, they'd be either dead or captured, her mission a failure.

Beth wasn't formally in command of the three civilians, but they were following what she wanted to do. It was her decision to let Dr. Moran rest up, and if it weren't for Randy, that decision would have resulted in disaster.

She glanced over to the man who was puffing as he carried the all-important case just behind Moran and her. His foresight had saved them. Randy wasn't a Wimmerman employee. He was a facilities maintenance man for PPY Transport, and when he'd fled, he'd helped himself to whatever he could carry that he thought would help. Among that haul were motion sensors. He'd doubled back 500 meters along their trail from the bluff where they'd slept the night before, placing one of the sensors for early warning. In the effort to get moving the next morning, he'd forgotten it until they were underway, and it made no sense to go back and retrieve it.

Thank goodness for that.

The abandoned sensor kicked off while they were at the terraforming site. A dozen somethings were moving past the sensor, somethings in the 500 kg range.

Crystals.

It could be coincidence, but Beth knew it wasn't. They were tracking whoever had killed one of their own.

They had to run, which was easier said than done. Beth and Whisper picked up the case between them, and with Moran alongside them and Randy bringing up the rear, they hurried to the road and started west. If the crystals were tracking them, then going through the woods wouldn't help shake them and would only slow them down.

To determine if that was the case, Randy emplaced his last sensor just beyond the entrance to the terraforming station.

The four made it less than a klick. Whisper and Beth dropped the case twice, much to the consternation of Moran. It was just too heavy, and the two women couldn't seem to walk in step, sometimes working against each other. Randy gave his .380 to Whisper, the geoloc to Beth, then heaved the case onto his shoulder, head canted uncomfortably to the side.

Beth felt horrible that she and Whisper couldn't handle the case, but there'd be time for self-recrimination later. What mattered now was to get away.

Moran, who'd started off with a burst of energy, started flagging soon after Randy had taken over the case. Beth knew his reserves had been about depleted, so she took it upon herself to be his personal goad. She'd cajole, beg, yell . . . whatever it took to keep him moving.

They'd managed just two klicks when the sensor Randy had left at the station went off. Not only did it confirm the crystals were on their trail, but that they were closing fast.

Now, as Beth tried to drag Moran along, they'd probably cut the distance another 500 meters. Give them ten or fifteen more minutes, and they'd catch up.

"Where we going?" Beth asked Randy. "They'll be here soon."

"Orcville is just up ahead. The crystals cleared it out, but maybe we can lose them in amongst the village, or better yet, find a boat."

"A boat?"

"Yeah, the village is on the Avon. The crystals, they've got their own boats to transport ore down to Lockleaze, but they don't seem to like water much. Probably too heavy to float."

Which could be true. Or water, which was part oxygen, after all, was poisonous to them, or they could be alien cats that just didn't like to get wet.

It didn't matter why, only that the crystals might avoid it, and Beth was more than willing to grasp at any straw. It beat the feeling of helplessness that there was nothing she could do.

"You hear that?" she asked Moran. "Just up ahead. Push it."

"I'm trying," Moran whined.

Beth felt a twitch of compassion and started to reassure him, but she cut that off short. Compassion might get them all killed. She had to be the tough taskmaster if she was going to have any hope in getting Moran and his case off the planet.

"Don't just try. Do it!"

As they started to round a bend in the road, Beth spotted a small house, maybe 50 or 60 square meters. Beyond that, through the trees, Beth could see more buildings.

Randy groaned, but Beth didn't know if that was because he was reaching his endurance limit or he was relieved to have reached the village.

"We're here," she said for both men.

"They're coming!" Whisper shouted from where she trailed the three. She turned and sprinted forward to join them. "Move it, move it!"

Beth couldn't see around the bend, but she felt a surge of adrenaline. She half-led, half-dragged Moran forward and to the slope over the village proper.

In other circumstances, Orcville could be considered quaint and pretty. Thirty or forty white buildings, most with dark brown trim, made up the small village, while a long, graceful bridge crossed the river, heading north to the rest of the valley. The river itself was broad, brown water covered with islands of green floating hyacinth torn free by the spring rains. None of that registered with Beth, however. The total lack of life hinted at something nasty that had stripped the village of its residents.

If there was going to be a boat here, it would be down the hill and on the river, so Beth turned off the road, pulling Moran and scrambling down a planted verge and onto one of the village roads, one that looked like it might lead directly to the river's edge. Moran barely kept his feet, but beside them, Randy fell, dropping the case as they both tumbled to the road.

"Watch it, you idiot!" Moran shouted, pulling away from Beth and rushing to the case, which had fallen on its side.

He checked the indicator light, which displayed a steady green. He gave a huge sigh, tipped the case right-side up, then sunk to the ground, back to it, head tilted up and eyes closed.

"Sorry," Randy told Beth as he struggled to get back to his feet, breathing heavily. "I just lost it."

"No harm done. The light's still green, so don't worry about it," Beth said. "Now let's get down to the water."

Behind them, Whisper took three jumps down to reach them. "They're right behind me."

Beth pulled the protesting Moran to his feet while Randy picked up one side of case, lifted it half a meter, then dropped it. He was spent.

"Take him," Beth said, pushing Moran at him.

She set her legs, grabbed both handles, and reminding herself to lift with her legs, not her back, stood.

The case was heavy, but she managed to shuffle down the middle of the street taking short, choppy steps. She didn't know how long she could keep it up, but she'd get it down to the water somehow.

She made it two blocks, maybe 150 meters, before she had to put it down for a moment to catch her breath and shake out her hands. She was just about to lift it again when Whisper handed Randy back his Winchester-Simmons and pushed her aside. Whisper squatted, and then with a grunt, heaved it up to her head, tottering a few steps until she gained her equilibrium.

"Let's go," she managed to get out.

Beth felt guilty but grateful. She pulled Moran by the arm when Randy said, "There they are."

Beth turned. Three, then four crystals appeared at the side of the highway right where they'd scrambled down the verge. She expected them to shoot, or whatever FALs did, and cut them down, first feeling utter despair before that was quickly replaced by anger.

She drew her M-20 and yelled out, "Shoot them!" as she raised her handgun to fire.

Randy pushed her arm down, saying, "Not yet. They'll want to try and capture us first."

A small crystal machine trundled down the verge. At least she thought it was a machine, and not the FAL version of a bloodhound. It just *looked* mechanical. The four crystals in sight followed it, then two more appeared alongside the edge of the highway.

Don't stand here gawking, Floribeth. Move!

She spun and dragged Moran down the street at a jog. Whisper had already covered 20 or 30 meters, her legs in the stiff gait of someone carrying weight. Within moments, Beth and Moran were beside her, Randy just behind.

Loud clicking reached down the street from behind, louder than she'd heard before. Beth didn't know if the clicking was language or just the sounds of their bodies moving, but it served to give her more of a push. All she could think of was the river flowing past the village. There had to be a boat there, and she refused to consider the possibility that there wouldn't be one.

The road opened up into a small, artificially-cobblestoned square. A bar, a bakery, and a small store were along the sides, but Beth was focused on the platform on the end, chairs neatly lined up so that the villagers could sit and watch the river flow by.

The cobblestones might be visually appealing, but they made walking more difficult. There was nothing to do but push forward and hope Whisper could keep her feet.

"Keep going!" Randy shouted from behind them.

Something in his voice made Beth turn her head and look back.

He'd stopped at the entrance to the square. Just 25 meters past him, the crystals were advancing. Beth hadn't realized they were that close. They looked huge, dwarfing the puny human who dared to stand before them.

Randy raised his Winchester-Simmons and fired. A chunk of one of the FALs shattered while the rest immediately scattered.

Beth kept moving, but she couldn't turn away. Randy managed to fire one more round before several lances of light reached out and enveloped him. One moment he was standing there, the next, what was left of him fell to the ground.

Beth bit back a gasp as she looked forward again, sprinting to the edge of the viewing platform, fully expecting for the two of them to be shot with the same weapons. Whisper was at the edge, looking over. Beth took a step forward and followed her gaze. There was no boat.

"Get down there," Whisper said, pushing the container over the edge to where it landed with a splat in the mud that made up the river bank. Beth pushed an almost comatose Moran off the platform, then jumped after him, landing in knee-deep water, the current already pulling at her.

Whisper wasn't with them.

"Jump!" Beth called out.

"Just go. Float downstream. Be careful at Lockleaze."

"Help me get there!" Beth shouted, but Whisper had turned and was facing into the square. Facing the crystals.

"Help me free this," Beth yelled at Moran, fighting back the tears.

Moran was sitting in the mud, feet in the water, eyes glazed over.

"Damn it, help me!" Beth yelled again, jerking ferociously on the handle, trying to free the case from the mud's sucking grip.

On the fourth jerk, the case came free, sending Beth over on her ass in the river. That gave her a perfect view of Whisper as white crystal fingers shot out and enveloped her, like a moth in a spider's grip.

Beth scrambled to her feet, kicked the case out into the river's grasp, hoping it would float. She grabbed Moran by the collar and dragged him into the water, kicking to catch up to the case.

She took one look back, expecting to see the crystals appear at the edge of the platform, but the river was powerful, and within seconds, they were rushed past a building and out of sight.

Chapter 19

"You need to keep your head up, Doctor Moran," Beth said, reaching through the tangled hyacinth between them to pull up on his hair.

Moran opened his eyes, coughed, then gave Beth a rueful smile. "I know. Sorry. I'm just cold and tired. Hard to hang on."

Beth could sympathize. She was cold and tired, too. The Avon, which had seemed warm when they entered it, had sapped their body heat. But they had to keep hanging tough if they were going to make it out alive and with the baby crystal.

Beth's left hand had been locked around the case's handle so long that she wondered if she'd be able to release it if they got that far. Luckily, the thing just floated, the top a centimeter or so above the surface of the water. She wasn't under any illusion that she could keep both the case and her afloat at the same time. If it weren't for the hyacinth, they'd both have probably drowned now, that or crawled out onto the shore with no real way to get Moran and the case back to the *Tala*.

As usual, Beth had no idea why the terraforming engineers had included water hyacinths in the mix for New Bristol. Maybe they kept the water clean or something. This time, however, she wanted to go back in time and kiss them. As on Earth, the hyacinths broke free in large rafts during the spring rains and floated downstream and out into the ocean, an event that took place for about a month. For once, the stars were aligned, and this happened to be during that period.

The raft Beth had pulled Moran and the case into was roughly five meters by four. Not the biggest raft, but more than enough to conceal them. Concealment wasn't the only benefit. While they were not buoyant enough to completely support a person, they did provide some buoyancy that helped the two float. By clinging to the stalks, they could try and relax, their faces out of the water.

It's hard to relax when I'm shivering.

She was worried about Moran. He'd been quiet over the last hour, and this had been the third time she'd had to jostle him to alertness.

"Try to come closer to me so I can hang onto you," Beth told him.

"What, so I can drag you down, too? No, you keep a hold of that case. You've got to get it back, at least."

"My orders are to get you back, too, sir."

"That's what's important, not me. That little baby is your priority."

"I'll get you back. I promise, sir."

He gave a small chuckle, then said, "A big promise, one that you might not be able to keep. Night's falling, and I'll be honest. I don't know if I can hang on that long."

"Don't say that, Doctor Moran. You can do it."

He was quiet for a moment, then said, "We've become pretty close over this day. Hell, you depantsed me."

Beth gave a little chuff. It was true. Trying to help him stay afloat, she'd tried something taught in water training. She'd pulled off his pants, tied the feet closed, then sunk her head under the water and exhaled through the waist to create a float for him. It worked, but she had to re-inflate it every four or five minutes, which had become exhausting. Already cold after an hour in the water, the two had missed the handoff of his pants to her, and now they were on the bottom of the Avon somewhere.

"Given that, don't you think 'Doctor Moran' is a little formal?"

"Sir?"

"Why don't you call me Lex?"

She pulled apart some of the hyacinths to get a better look at his face. His eyes were closed, his chin just clear of the water.

"OK, Lex. I'll do that. I'm Beth, by-the-way."

****

Three hours later, in full darkness, they reached Lockleaze. It wasn't ablaze in lights as she'd expected. There were some lights across the city, but it was mostly a black nothingness in the dark.

There was activity, however. Several of the crystal boats had passed the two in the water, each time Beth sinking as low as she could to avoid detection. The boats, which looked like futuristic barges, never slowed down. For all Beth knew, they were unmanned.

Here closer to the city, the boats were more densely packed. Passing the refinery, they were stacked out in the water, the closest to the shore alive with activity, the sounds reaching across the water. Beth couldn't see well enough to tell if that was crystals or some sort of automated machinery.

According to Whisper, there were tens of thousands, maybe more, humans in the city, most around the refinery. Beth hoped there were. It was too disheartening to consider that the city, once home to 240,000 people, was now a ghost town.

With a numb hand, she pulled up her geoloc, which she'd long ago tied to her flightsuit, afraid she'd drop it in the water. She knew where she was and how far they had to go, but she had to see it on the display.

"Thirty-eight more klicks, Lex," she whispered.

Lex didn't answer.

****

Shortly after dawn, the eastern sky a light rose, Lex gave a sigh and slipped beneath the surface of the river.

"Oh, no, you don't," Beth shouted aloud, angry at herself for losing concentration.

She ripped her hand, now a wrinkled claw, away from the case and ducked under the raft. The water was brown with sediment, so even had it been broad daylight, she wouldn't have been able to see a thing. She had to go by touch. She thrashed under the hyacinth, which held her back, making her want to scream with frustration. But the same mass of vegetation kept Lex from sinking just long enough for a questing finger to brush him. With a lunge, she had his shirt in her right hand. Five good kicks, and she pushed their heads up through the hyacinths and into the air.

She took three huge breaths, then turned to Lex. He couldn't have been under for more than 20 seconds, even if it had seemed much longer, but he wasn't breathing. Treading water, Beth pulled him around, locked her mouth on his, and gave three quick puffs. Nothing. This wasn't the best position to give mouth-to-mouth resuscitation, but there was no other option. She gave four more, putting everything she had into it, and to her immense surprise and relief, he coughed, a weak trickle of water dripping out of his mouth.

Thank you, Lord, she offered a little prayer, relieved that he hadn't breathed in half of the river.

"The case," she said in a panic, looking around for it. But it was still there, held in place by the hyacinths. She gave a sigh of relief and turned back to Lex.

He wasn't in the clear. He weakly coughed a few more times, breathing shallowly. Beth considered leaving the raft for the shore, but she could see several facilities coming right down to the river's edge. She didn't know how many crystals would be in the area, and she thought it would be just too dangerous. And, truth be told, she knew that if she got out of the river, she might never get back in, choosing to try overland, and knowing she'd fail.

But she had to do something. His body was stone cold. He could die from hypothermia. She considered her options, then with one arm around him, she used the other to reach down and unhook her survival kit. The kit was designed for someone with the use of only one hand to open, but that assumed a hand that hadn't been in cold water for twenty hours. She finally managed to get it open, losing some of the contents to the river, but not the monofilament line. Using her teeth to hold it, she horsed Lex around until his back was to her. Pulling him in tight, she wrapped the line the best she could, until his back was flush against her front. Beth used the entire length, running it through his shirtsleeves and her flight suit flaps. It was slow going, but after a good ten minutes, Lex was secured against her. Hopefully, her body heat would keep him alive, and his weight wouldn't drown them both. She had to tread water to keep them both up, her legs kicking his.

It wasn't optimal, but it was the only thing she could think of.

"You should have let me go," Lex whispered, almost too soft for her to hear, and the first time he'd spoken in hours.

"No, I shouldn't have. And quit talking like that."

He sighed, and for a moment, Beth thought he'd drifted off again.

"Tell my wife . . ." he started, before trailing off.

"Tell her what?" Beth prompted.

"If I don't make it, and after you free the planet, find my wife and tell her."

Beth wanted to protest about him not making it, but she knew this was important. "Tell your wife what?"

"Ryan. It was him. He got the crystal."

"Ryan? Who's Ryan?"

There was a long pause, then, "Ryan's our son. He was my assistant. Once we figured out that they were growing babies, we knew we had to get one."

There was another pause, and Beth was going to nudge him again when he said, "We designed the case together, and when it was time, I wanted to go, but I'm old, and he's not. He had to go.

"He did it. I don't know how, but my boy did it. Cost him his life, it did, though. But he got it back to me first." There was another pause, then, "It should have been me."

Beth tread water in shock, letting it sink in. Now she knew why Lex hadn't wanted to talk about how he'd gotten the infant crystal. It was a mixture of guilt and grief. It also explained why he'd kept telling her that the case was what was important, not him. Anything else would negate what his son had done.

"Tell her," Lex said, his voice barely a whisper.

"I will."

****

Thirty-eight hours after they'd entered the water, Beth, her legs like lead from hours of treading water, drew upon every milligram of energy she had and swam Lex and the case ashore. With night closing in on them, she pulled the unconscious Lex out of the water and struggled mightily to drag him through the mud and onto dry land, leaving him under some brush before returning for the case.

She pulled the case through the shore mud, grunting with each heave that moved it half a meter each time. Once, her feet slipped forward, and she sat on the mud, staring stupidly at the case in the dark before she was able to gather

her wits, stand, and try again. It took ten minutes, but she finally reached Lex.

All energy spent, she fell face-first in the ground and passed out.

Chapter 20

Beth groaned and turned her head. She ached, and she wasn't ready to get up.

Just twenty more minutes, she bargained with herself. *Just twenty.*

She started to slide back down into the embrace of sleep. Something was off, but she was too tired to figure it out until it hit her.

"Lex!" she shouted and sat up, her heart racing.

Doctor Lex Moran lay next to her, his face in the dirt. He wasn't moving. In a panic, Beth reached over and pulled him to her, afraid of what she'd find.

Lex was alive, but not in good shape. He was cold and barely breathing, his chest rising and falling almost too slightly to notice. But breathing shallowly was better than not breathing at all. Beth fell back to a sitting position and tried to clear her mind and take stock of the situation.

They were by the river, the immense flow unconcerned whether the planet was held by humans or crystals. There were tracks and churned-up mud in the riverbank where she'd dragged Lex and the specimen case out of the water, tracks that might as well have been neon signs pointing them out to anyone looking.

Her memory was somewhat vague about reaching the end of their river journey. She was sure she'd hidden the two of them and the case pretty well, but daylight told a different story. They were partially under a small bush, but rather exposed from the river or to anyone walking by. She was going to have to rectify that.

Her tongue felt like it was covered in felt. She tried to scrape it off against her top teeth, but that didn't do much good. She looked back at the river, wondering if she should risk it. She'd lost her purification straw sometime during the night, and now she was thirsty. The chance of getting something nasty was too great, however, and she decided against it.

At least she had her geoloc, which was still attached to her flightsuit. Suddenly afraid that she'd misread it during the night and they still had klicks to go, she hesitated before turning on the display. She'd worried needlessly. She'd come out right where she'd planned after they entered the river upstream. The *Tala*, hopefully repaired, should be just a little over three klicks away.

"Lex, can you walk?" she asked. "Lex?"

Dr. Moran didn't twitch.

Beth picked up his wrist and felt a rapid and reedy pulse. She wasn't a doctor, but she knew that wasn't good, just as she knew Lex wasn't about to suddenly recover and make the trek.

She briefly considered carrying the unconscious man, but after struggling to pick him up, realized that was a no-go as well. Beth gave a quick glance at the case. She might be able to pick it up, but in her weakened state, she knew for a fact that she couldn't carry it three klicks.

There was only one thing to do: she had to stash Lex and the case, then go get help.

She didn't know if the crystals would have been able to track her to this spot, or if they had patrols on the river, but she didn't think leaving the mud marked up like that was a good idea. She broke off a branch, then did her best to smooth out the mud, throwing water from the river on it as well. It wasn't great—it wasn't even good—but it might be better than what it was before.

The next thing to do was to move Lex and the case. The edge of the forest was only 20 meters farther, so Beth dragged first Lex, then the case over and under what looked to be some type of laurel. It was more difficult to get Lex and the case inside of the thicket than to it, but she felt reasonably confident that they would escape casual notice.

"I'm coming back," Beth told Lex. "Just hang in there."

The laurel made the going rough for the first 50 meters, but then it thinned out. She made good time walking through the woods, expecting something to go wrong with every step. For once, however, luck shone upon her, and in and hour-and-a-twenty minutes, she was looking across the road to the maintenance shack where the *Tala* was taken what seemed to be months before.

There was no sign of life. After all she'd gone through, Beth couldn't fail simply because she was too eager, so she sat in the undergrowth for a full 30 minutes, watching and waiting. She saw or heard nothing.

She couldn't wait much longer. Either Horace and Yeti were there with the *Tala*, or they weren't. She had to find out.

Beth crept to the edge of the highway, then stood and darted across, taking shelter behind a large tree. She stood there for a long minute, trying to determine if she'd been spotted. When there was no outcry, no flurry of crystal clicks, she quietly picked her way through the forest litter to the back of the building.

She stood, back against the rear of the building, listening for any sign of life . . . human or crystal. Once again, nothing.

There were several windows along the back, one just a few meters away. Beth crept up to it, then slowly leaned her head around so she could see in. With the morning sun, the glare was too bright, so she brought up a hand to cup it around the window to look in again.

"About time you showed up," Horace yelled as a door down the wall slammed open. "We'd about given up on you. Where's Whisper and Randy?"

"Mother of God," Beth muttered, crossing herself as she tried to still her nerves. "About gave me a heart attack."

She stepped away from the wall and said, "I'll tell you everything later. Right now, I need your help."

Horace looked at her for a moment, frowning as he took in her disheveled appearance, then looked back inside the building and shouted, "Yeti, come here. The pilot needs us."

He looked back up at Beth as Yeti joined him and said, "Lead on."

Chapter 21

Despite their questions, Beth hadn't explained the situation to Horace and Yeti as she led them back to where she'd stashed Lex and the case, suddenly afraid that something would have happened to them while she was gone. But they were both there, Lex looking like he hadn't moved a centimeter.

None of the three of them were prime physical specimens. Beth was probably in the best shape normally, but she'd been driven to the end of her rope. Between Horace, Yeti, and her, however, they managed to get Lex and the case back to the maintenance shack, even if it took them three hours. Lex was completely out if it, so Yeti arranged some blankets on the floor where they lay him. Horace kept looking at the case with curiosity, but Beth left him in the dark. She had no idea if the crystals interrogated prisoners, but on the off-chance that they did, better safe than sorry. Whisper was already captured, and for all Beth knew, they could be torturing her for information.

Which was all the more reason to get off the planet now. But Lex needed rest and recovery. Escaping the planet's gravity well could kill him if she tried it in his condition.

"Try and get something down his throat," Beth told Yeti before she finally turned to her baby, the *Tala*, sitting in the middle of the machine shop.

Beth's heart skipped a beat. Her beautiful fighter was . . . *wasn't* beautiful anymore, to put it mildly. Her fuselage was torn up aft of the cockpit, far more than it had been before. and a boxlike contraption was sticking out of the damage like a tumor. There were scrapes along her entire side, as if she'd been sideswiped in an accident. One of the scrapes ran right across the X-1000 cloaking bulb in the bow.

She looked at Horace. If the *Tala* couldn't fly, or if she couldn't evade detection, then the entire trip down the river would have been wasted. Randy's death and Whisper's capture would have been in vain.

"Does this still work?" Beth asked, running her hand over the small cloaking bulb, starting with that as she was afraid to ask the big question.

"I checked. I'm not sure how the system works, but nothing looks damaged," Horace told her.

Just ask the real question, Floribeth!

"Can she fly?" she asked, her voice catching.

"She'll fly," Horace said. "I mean, I think she will. She should."

Beth heaved a sigh of relief.

"Not so well in the atmosphere, though. You're going to have to take it easy."

"How easy? I need to be able open her up if the FALs get on my tail."

He considered the question, then said, "I don't rightly know, to be honest. I don't have the right equipment here to run the simulations. I've done the calculations, and while my little addition now works the starboard control surfaces, it does it much, much slower. That won't matter at low speeds, but once you start getting up to Mach, my box there will be interfering with your aerodynamics too much, and the control system I gyvered for you won't be able to keep up."

"Luckily, your plane is a flying rock."

"Luckily? What do you mean?"

"He means, you get by mostly with power," Yeti said, joining them. "If this were some high-efficiency plane, then the modifications we did would result in an unstable aircraft. It couldn't manage more than a few seconds of flight."

What Yeti said made absolutely no sense to her, but if they said it would fly, then she had to trust them in that.

"Once you're in space, then you're home free," Horace added.

Beth knew that from a theoretical standpoint, but she was used to her beautiful and sleek Wasp, and she had to make sure.

"So, if I have to goose her up there, I can max her out?"

"Sure. Aerodynamics, or lack thereof, mean nothing in a vacuum, Horace assured her.

She just had to figure out how to get a crippled Wasp into space without attracting attention. At the moment, however, she was too tired, physically and mentally, to give it much thought.

"There is one other problem, though," he said, frowning.

"What?"

If the *Tala* could get her to the gate, then that was what mattered. Anything else was minor.

"The round that hit you took out your comms. I don't have anything to replace it with."

OK, not so minor.

"But I pulled data after I landed," Beth said.

"From the AI. Which has a built-in redundancy. Well, the comms has the same redundancy," he added as an afterthought.

"So, why doesn't it work, then?"

"Well, you've got two comms suites. Both work. But they're funneled here," he said, pointing to a spot beside the box he'd attached to the fuselage, "and then to the array. Your suites are working, but the array won't send it anywhere. If you're close enough, the suite itself will pick up and even transmit."

"How close?" Beth asked, fearing the answer.

"A couple of klicks. Maybe ten."

Which was nothing in space.

Beth rubbed her eyes as she tried to clear her brain.

Beth was long overdue, and whoever would be waiting for her outside each of the three possible gates would probably be long gone by now, assuming her mission was a bust. Hopefully, there would be someone there. If not, she'd have to manage her own subsequent gate passage, which was always a last option.

Her mind wasn't coming up with a nice, neat solution. It remained blank. She needed some sleep, and maybe she'd come up with something after that.

At least the *Tala* would fly. That was the big thing. She'd work out the comms later. Beth gave her Wasp a last pat, then walked over to where Lex was laid out and took a spot beside him.

"Wake me up in a couple of hours, OK?" she asked.

Fifteen seconds later, she was out.

****

"I don't see why I have to be on the bottom," Lex muttered, for the moment relatively lucid.

"You're bigger than I am," Beth said.

True, but that wasn't the only reason she wanted Lex strapped into the seat. She wasn't going to mention the second reason to him, however.

She looked across the cockpit to Horace, who gave a shrug, a pained smile on his face. He might be a skilled engineer, but this was well beyond his scope.

Beth had been squirreled away with Yeti and him for almost thirty-three local hours—about thirty-seven standard hours. A good portion of that had been asleep, recovering from her ordeal. Now, with Lex conscious—mostly—and with both of them fed and Lex given a pair of work pants from the gear locker, it was time to go. She'd like to have Lex in better condition, but she felt vulnerable, and the key to her mission was in the case now in the compartment where her P-13 hadron canon had once been. As long as that made it back, that took precedence over either one of them.

She'd been ready to go since she woke up but decided to wait until dark. There was still no indication that darkness gave pilots any advantage over the crystals, but there was no indication that it didn't, either. Now, three hours after sundown, it was time to go.

With Horace's help, they managed to strap Lex into the cockpit. He struggled for a moment, then slipped back into sleep.

It was time for her to climb aboard, too, but she looked up at Horace and said, "Thank you. None of this would be possible if not for you and Yeti."

He gave a shrug, then said, "Or Whisper, or Randy. Or you."

Beth had crashed for a solid four hours the day before, but after waking and getting some food inside of her, she told Yeti and him what had transpired. The two had experienced an alien invasion, they'd certainly lost friends and family, but they had taken her news of Randy and Whisper hard, especially Horace. Beth wondered if simply surviving an invasion created the same sort of bonds that people who faced combat together formed. From their reactions, she'd guess yes.

"If you see any of their people, you know, after, then let them know both sacrificed themselves for the greater good."

Beth almost winced as she said the words. "The greater good" was what all the politicians said after sending people to die on distant worlds or in the blackness of space. The fact that it was true didn't matter to her. It just sounded canned to her.

"I will. Just you make sure there is an after for us here. Get whatever that is back to folks who can make use of it," Horace said.

She opened her mouth to reply, but then realized it had all been said. She nodded, then climbed into the cockpit, twisting around to slide her legs forward. She had to bend her knees as she sat on top of Lex, but she fit.

Barely.

It was awkward. She was almost supine, and she was missing the familiar embrace of her harness. She had to tuck her chin to her chest in order to see the display. There was probably a way to shift the display farther up to the main part of the canopy, but if there was, she'd long forgotten how to do it. For a moment, she was tempted to delay her take off and ask Horace to figure it out, but she realized if she got to the point where she had to make full use of her display, then she wasn't going to survive anyway, not with the repairs Horace had made.

"OK, I'm in. You two get out of here now. I'll give you ten minutes to get clear."

Ten minutes were probably overkill. She'd be taking off at a fraction of the *Tala's* power, so anything past 30 or 40 meters should be OK. But if there was a surge of propulsion somehow, she didn't want to fry the two people who'd made the takeoff possible.

"Got it. We'll be long gone by then," he said.

Yeti was already at the door. Beth had said her goodbye before she and Horace got Lex into the *Tala*, but she raised a hand and waved. Yeti returned it and shouted, "Fair winds and following seas," the farewell sailors had been giving each other for thousands of years.

"Keep your head down, you hear?" Beth shouted back.

She settled in farther, skootching her butt between Lex's legs, then closed the canopy, which ended up just a few centimeters from her nose.

"This is going to be tight," she muttered.

Lex was smaller than Bull, with whom she'd shared the *Tala I's* cockpit, but she had been pretty much out of it then, and the trip was still somewhat fuzzy. Now, she was extremely aware of the tiny space and Lex under her. Something, maybe his belt, was digging into the small of her back.

Should of thought of that before.

There wasn't any way to turn around and take care of that, so it was just something to be endured. She forced it out of her mind.

Horace and Yeti left the building, and Beth started her timer. Wasps took off in close proximity of people all the time, but from pads or hangars specifically designed to protect people. The maintenance shed had none of those safeguards, so she was being uber-conscious. Still, as she looked out of the open sliding cargo door, half-expecting to see crystal soldiers appearing, she started feeling anxious. She wanted to get going. She'd gone too far to have the mission fail now.

The mission. What had been the chances of success? Twenty-nine percent, the CNO had said. She could see the light at the end of the tunnel. Now she just had to traverse that tunnel successfully.

Her mission was the key, but she still wished she'd seen something, anything, to indicate how the crystals had destroyed Portland. After much internal debate, she'd told Horace and Yeti what had happened to the planet. They were shocked and rightfully concerned, but she asked them to spread the word however they could for others to keep their eyes peeled for anything that could reveal how the FALs managed to destroy a planet. She'd told them she'd try to see if the Navy could slip a message drone of some sort onto the planet and to this maintenance shed.

Beth didn't know if that was even possible. The *Tala's* cloaking depended upon the power output of her FC engine. A simple drone might not have the power to run the system.

Ten minutes is nothing in the sidereal of the universe, but it seemed like it stretched forever. But finally, her timer reached zero, and she gave the verbal order for the *Tala* to power up. Her display went to full active mode, the warm-up trees going through their steps. One by one, the flashing lights settled to green. Beth didn't know how she would handle in flight, but the AI thought the Wasp was ready.

She ran a second check on the flight control surfaces. There were some readings that were off, but nothing outside of the accepted parameters. Horace had already taken the *Tala* this far, so Beth was expecting no less, but still, that was a good sight.

"You ready, Lex?" she asked.

Her passenger mumbled something and shifted his body under her. She was going to take that as a yes—not that a no at this point was going to make a difference.

Beth was a hands-on pilot. She liked manual control. But with the *Tala's* interfaces beneath Lex, she was going to have to go verbal. The Tala's AI did all the actual flying either way, but Beth thought manual control left less room for error. She was always afraid of misspeaking. The AI's were designed with an intuitive pilot interface that took all factors into consideration, so misspeaking couldn't crash a fighter, but still, when milliseconds could be the difference between splashing an enemy fighter and getting splashed, Beth preferred every advantage.

Now, she had no choice, so she pulled out her silver cross, kissed it, and gave the order for the *Tala* to lift off. She barely felt the *Tala* rising. Slowly, the fighter floated across the floor toward the cargo doors.

"Floated" was almost a too-gentle term. It took a lot of power to suspend a Wasp a few feet above the deck and traverse in any direction. The same vectored thrusters that made a Wasp so maneuverable in space provided the thrust, but they were quite inefficient in this mode. Luckily, the *Tala's* FC engine had power to spare.

Debris and dust filled the shop as the *Tala* crept forward. Beth's fingers itched to be on the controls, but with Horace's repairs to the starboard control surfaces, the AI was once again more than capable enough to fly the Wasp out, and a moment later, the *Tala* emerged into the darkness of New Bristol's night. Beth gave one last check of the X-1000, which still showed green.

"It's make or break time, Lex," she said as she gave the order for the *Tala* to lift for space.

****

The departure from the planet's gravity well was anticlimactic. Keeping the thrust low, she slowly climbed through the atmosphere, every second expecting fighters, missiles, or something to knock her out of the sky. They'd managed to shoot her down once, after all.

But through luck or the new cloaking, she escaped detection. It had been a long, nerve-wracking trip of over two hours instead of the minutes it would have taken under normal conditions, but the *Tala* was now safely in space, heading to the secondary commercial gate.

Of course, if she kept up like this, the trip to the gate would take almost eight months. Neither Lex nor she would survive the journey. Not that she didn't consider it. The crystal baby, snug in its case in the P-13 compartment, theoretically would make it, and that was the most important thing to get in the hands of the science-types. But eight months was a long time during a war, and they needed it back sooner. No, Beth was going to have to bring the *Tala* up to speed and hope she'd remain undetected, or if she was detected, she could outrun any pursuit.

Beth went over her route again. She had adjusted the route to avoid, as much as possible, the concentrations of activity. There wasn't a clear shot to the gate (although it was much better than the route to the main commercial gate or the military gate), and if those blips on her display were crystal fighters, they could cut her off if they pierced her cloaking. But this gave her the best chance.

She involuntarily twitched her shoulders. Her back and neck itched. Beth was used to weightlessness. Lex evidently was not. He'd heaved shortly after reaching space, splattering against her neck, and without her helmet, which was too big to wear with both of them in the cockpit, some of it got inside the collar of her flightsuit. The *Tala* sensed the vomitus and sucked it out of the air, but that did nothing for what was on her.

She wasn't sure how it had reached her back, and maybe it was her imagination, but no matter. It itched.

"OK, Lex, I'm engaging the V-thirty. That is what we use in space for propulsion. We'll be accelerating at thirty-five G's, but the compensators will kick in, so you won't be crushed. There will be a . . . well, a ripple, some people call it, pass through your body as the compensators take effect, so be ready for it."

And don't throw up again, please.

"You OK?"

Lex muttered something and raised his hand past Beth's hip in a thumbs up.

"Here we go," she said before giving the commands to the fighter.

The *Tala* started to surge ahead. Beth felt the familiar grasp of the compensators. Lex squirmed under her, but thankfully didn't vomit again. With five-and-a-half hours to the gate, then who knew how long on the other side, she didn't fancy having more of Lex's stomach contents splattered across her.

Beth kept her eyes glued to the display. The combat AI would let her know if any of the contacts reacted to her, but she trusted herself more than a bunch of electrons. But there didn't seem to be any reaction as the *Tala* sped up and started making significant progress.

The key was when the Wasp reached a .10 C and higher, and that wouldn't take long. The *Tala* herself might be cloaked, but she'd be leaving a bow-wake as her passage disturbed the dust, neutrinos, cosmic rays, and magnetic fields that filled the "empty" space. The higher her speed, the more pronounced the wake.

"Is there anything to drink here?" Lex croaked out, breaking Beth's focus on her display.

"Uh, yeah. See the nipple to your right? That's for drinks and food. Just grab it in your mouth. It will automatically start dispensing. Do you want hot or cold?"

"Cold, please."

"Activate nutritional dispenser four," she ordered.

She could feel him shift under her, and a moment later, he said, "Thanks. That's better."

Beth wished he hadn't asked for the drink because now she realized how thirsty she was herself. She could probably twist her body around so she was face down on him, but that would be pretty awkward and would have her back bent uncomfortably, so she put it off for now.

She went back to her display, chin sunk on her chest so she could see it, which was pretty uncomfortable in and of itself. Still no reaction from the FALs.

You just keep doing what you're doing. Nothing here at all.

On her display, the purple triangle representing the gate looked so close. She just had to get to it.

"My legs are asleep," Lex said from beneath her.

Beth settled down a little farther, then lifted on his knees. That brought her knees up against the bottom of the display. At least that gave her a slightly better angle to it. She stared at the purple triangle as if she could will the distance to close.

She shouldn't have been surprised that she drifted off to sleep. Her body had been put through a lot, and it reacted as nature intended it to.

****

The alarm chime jolted her awake.

"Potential enemy activity," the AI droned.

Beth shook her head to get rid of the cobwebs, then ducked her chin to see the display. The *Tala* had made it about half-way to the gate. More urgently, a flight of eight craft of some kind had turned to face her route ahead.

"Probability that they are going to intercept me?" Beth asked.

"Seventy-nine percent."

"Crap," she muttered.

"What is it?" Lex asked, his voice bordering on panic. "Who is intercepting us?"

"It's the crystals. Hold on for a moment," she said, not having time to soothe the man at the moment.

"With the current acceleration profile, will they intercept?" she asked the AI over Lex's shout of "Crystals?"

Beth could see with her own eyes. She was seeing the enemy turn toward her about four minutes after they would have made it. She could estimate a track pretty well with her bare eyes based on that. But she wanted confirmation.

"Given assumed capabilities, yes."

Not a probability, Beth noted, but a flat "yes."

"Recalculate with the *Tala* at 50Gs acceleration."

The projected track changed. If the crystals accelerated at the rates they'd previously exhibited, then they would not be able to cut off the *Tala* before she shot the gate.

However, they'd be within both torpedo and their energy canon's range. Not point-blank range, but well within their effective range.

That's that.

"Begin acceleration to 60 Gs," she ordered.

"Sixty Gs requires Enhanced Force Measures," the AI said.

She could hear the slightly different tone as the engine sent more power to the thrust.

"What's happening? What's going on?" Lex shouted as he struggled beneath her.

"Lex!" she shouted, but he kept screaming.

Beth brought her knees higher against the canopy, then slammed down hard until he gave a woof and gasped for breath.

"Lex! Listen up. We've got crystals on our tails, but we can outrun them if we go into max drive. But our bodies can't handle the Gs without assistance. I'm about to administer G-shot to you. It's going to hurt like hell, and you're going to need rehab on the other side, but it's your only chance to make it through alive.

If you even make it Lex. Your body is already weak.

"No! Don't do it! I forbid you!" he shouted, but too late. She'd already initiated G-shot, the four injectors coming out of the seat, finding the four entrance arteries, and starting the process.

And this was the second reason why she'd put him in beneath her in the seat. G-shot was administered by the seat itself. It needed contact with the body.

"Ahh! Fuck!" he shouted. "Stop it! Stop it!"

Beth had gone through G-shot four times, and she knew what he was going through. She didn't have time for pity or calming words, though. Already, she was feeling the effects of heavy Gs. The compensators were working overtime, but they just couldn't keep up.

"Lower cockpit temperature to five degrees Celsius," she ordered.

It probably wouldn't make a difference, but some studies showed low temperatures could help mitigate the damage done by excess G forces. Beth knew that she was signing her death warrant by ordering 60 Gs, but she was a stubborn soul, and she wasn't going to go down quietly.

She reached into her survival pack and pulled out the emergency beacon. She'd almost trashed it on New Bristol, and now, it could be the mission's savior. She armed and turned it on.

If the crystals wondered what her bow wake signaled, there would be no question now. With the *Tala's* comms down, however, Beth had to make sure that the Wasp could be found once she shot the gate.

The edges of her vision began to turn musty as she approached gray-out, and she crossed herself before grunting out half-a-dozen AGSMs, Anti-G Straining Maneuvers, that pushed the gray back. Lex had fallen into quiet moans underneath her, but she ignored him, needing to make one last check. The *Tala* was heading for the gate, and she'd make it if there were no unseen surprises. The FALs would undoubtedly take her under fire, but the *Tala* was on a 90% speed, 10% maneuver profile. She'd maneuver to protect herself from torpedoes or energy canon fire, but the priority went to straight-line speed. Immediately upon shooting the gate, the acceleration would be cut, then a gradual deceleration on the other side.

Everything looked correct—and out of her control now. Either the *Tala* was going to be able to shoot the gate or not.

Beth felt the Gs in waves, now, each one pushing on her chest harder and harder. The compensator was spiking and dipping as it tried to keep her alive.

She tried to fight G-Loc with continual AGSMs, but it was like holding back a flood with a broom. The gray spread back across her eyesight with a vengeance, and breathing became just too hard to do.

The last thing Beth saw was the purple triangle of the gate on her display before all went dark.

POITIER NAVAL HOSPITAL, GANYMEDE STATION

Epilogue

Beth opened her eyes, then immediately closed them. She should be used to waking up in hospitals by now, but it was just as jarring as it had been the first time. Her mind was fuzzy as she tried to put back the pieces of the puzzle.

"Well, we're back among the living," a voice said to her left.

Beth turned her head slightly and was rewarded with a piercing pain that lanced from the top of her head down into her gut. She gave a little intake of air, and the pain faded to a heavy throbbing.

She slowly opened one eye to see a Navy nurse rise from a chair at the side of the room, put down her pad, and walk up to the side of the bed.

"Take it easy there, Petty Officer. You've had quite an experience," she said, leaning over to look at the readings. "Oh, I can see you've got a wicked headache. Let me help with that."

She entered something into the control, and a moment later, relief flooded through Beth. Whatever it was, she liked it.

"What happened?" Beth asked as the immediate pain faded.

"Well, you need to tell me. Us. We're all curious. I mean, you're a medical mystery, after all."

"Mystery?"

"Yes, I should say so. All we know is that you were recovered in your Wasp, and if the instruments are correct, you survived an equivalence of 14.7 G's for thirty-one minutes. That's a record, we think, and every doctor here at Poitier wants to poke and prod you to figure out how."

"Fourteen-point-seven? But I had her up to sixty Gs," Beth said as the memory started to come back.

"That's the equivalence. You may have had it up to sixty, but your compensator took care of most of that. Still a rather remarkable thing."

More and more came flooding back. A compensator was designed to handle 40 Gs, but she remembered the pulsing as if it kept trying, pushing itself. She'd given the G-shot to Lex so she . . .

"Lex! Did he make it?" she asked sitting up suddenly, then falling back.

"Who's Lex?" the nurse asked.

"The other man in the cockpit with me. Lex. Dr. Moran."

"You were in a Wasp, honey. That's a one-seater," she said, concern in her eyes as she put her palm on Beth's forehead.

"But—"

Whatever Beth was going to say was cut off when the door into the room flung open. A broad-shouldered man in a dark blue suit entered the room, followed by a female GT.

The muscle took the nurse gently by the upper arm and pulled her back while the GT said, "That will be all, Lieutenant. I'll handle this now."

The nurse's mouth dropped open, and she looked from the GT to Beth and back before stammering out, "She's my charge."

"And you will be back with her soon, but for now, I'm going to have to ask you to leave.

The muscle slowly, but firmly, led the nurse away.

"I'm going to report this to Doctor Singh!" she shouted as the door closed behind her.

The muscle looked back at the GT who gave a slight nod, and the man stepped out, leaving Beth and the GT alone.

"I know you," Beth said as the GT stepped up beside the bed. "You're a Tuominen. The one where I got my brief for the mission."

"Guilty as charged," she said. "Doctor Weet Tuominen, Fifth Directorate."

Beth widened her eyes at that. The Fifth Directorate was made up of spooks, spies, and all the people who made the Directorate function.

"What do you want from me?" Beth asked.

There were rumors of the 5D "disappearing" people when their continued breathing became problematic.

Dr. Tuominen smiled as if she could read Beth's concern, then said, "I'm just here to give you an update, then a few instructions. That's all.

"Your mission was, shall I say, a goat rope from the start. Isn't that how you put it in the Navy? We would have done it differently, but the Navy wanted their say, and since we needed their platform, we accepted their input."

"Ma'am?"

"Not your fault. Not the Navy's, either. But they think of taking the fight to the enemy, not how to get around them. But despite the inherent issues, you somehow managed to overcome them. We know what happened aboard your Wasp, and we've debriefed Doctor Moran—"

"So, he made it? I didn't know if he'd survive," Beth said, a wave of relief washing over her.

"He made it. Not in great condition, and angry that he was 'injected with a foreign substance,' as he put it. He's got a long convalescence, but he'll be fine.

"But to get back to you, I'd like to hear what happened from your perspective. I want it all."

"From when?" Beth asked.

"From entry into the atmosphere until you went into G-Loc," Dr. Tuominen said.

Beth took a moment to gather her thoughts, which were still a bit muddled, then went through the entire mission, trying to recall each detail. Dr. Tuominen never took notes, and she didn't have a visible recording device, but she listened intently, asking a few times for clarification or prompting Beth along.

When Beth told her about her instructions to Horace and Yeti concerning finding how the crystals were destroying planets, she said, "I can get something to the maintenance shed. We're already on that in the remaining captured worlds, but any intel could be valuable."

Of course, they're on it, Beth told herself. *They're 5D.*

Beth felt a little naive thinking that she, just a dumb fighter jock, could have somehow made a breakthrough figuring out such a major problem. 5D would have been dealing with that issue from the beginning.

It took almost an hour, but finally, Beth was finished, feeling like a sponge that had been squeezed dry.

"That was an amazing story," Dr. Tuominen said. "Very impressive. I'll be sending over a few techs to go over your actions again. They're the ones who'll have some specifics to ask you."

She hesitated a moment, a slight frown on her face, then she said, "But I have to ask you something. This is a little more personal, though, so you don't need to answer. I am just curious."

"Ma'am?"

"In your Wasp, when you gave Doctor Moran the G-shot. Why did you do that?"

"I don't understand, ma'am."

"I mean, you had to assume you were going to die."

Beth looked down at her hand as if just now noticing it. She flexed her fingers, marveling at the miracle of life.

"He was the mission, ma'am. That's all."

"Doctor Moran? Not to take away anything he and his son had done, but he wasn't the mission. We've debriefed him, and he wasn't able to offer anything new of value."

Beth's heart fell.

"So . . . so, the mission was a failure?" she said, her voice cracking.

"Failure?" Dr. Tuominen asked. "Not in the least. The mission was a resounding success."

"But you just said—"

"I said Doctor Moran wasn't able to offer anything new. But the . . . *equipment* . . . he—and you—brought back was invaluable."

"Was the equipment, uh, intact?" Beth asked.

"Extremely intact. And it is providing a wealth of information that will prove very beneficial in the war effort."

Beth didn't understand why they were speaking around the subject, but she could play along.

"I just wanted to know why you did that. I'd have hated to lose you, but I guess that's in keeping with what my brother told me about you."

That got Beth's attention. She looked up and asked, "You were the commander's sister?"

Dr. Tuominen nodded. "He was my little brother. Always the one with stars in his eyes," she said with a sigh.

"He was mighty impressed with you, which is one of the reasons the Director asked for you by name."

"What?" Beth asked. She could have been knocked over by a feather.

Why would the Director himself ask for her?

"Yes, you were ideally suited for the mission because of your size, and because of that, the Navy couldn't refuse. But it was your abilities, as my brother relayed them to me, that initiated the request. Once we knew we needed Navy help, you were the logical choice."

This was almost too much to comprehend. She was an enlisted pilot. A well-decorated one, to be sure, but she couldn't imagine her name being bandied about at the upper reaches of the government. By the Director, none-the-less.

"I just asked that because I was curious. I'm afraid that the idea of self-sacrifice isn't common among my peers."

Beth didn't know if by peers, she meant in the higher levels of the government or the Golden Tribe. Her brother, though, understood what it meant, however, when he took out the crystal mega-ship.

"You are a valuable member of the Navy, and you seem to have a knack of being at the center of major lodepoints. After Doctor Moran delivered the equipment to you, the logical choice was for you to live so you could fly your Wasp to safety. You wouldn't have had to rely on your emergency beacon to be recovered."

"So, that's what happened, ma'am? My beacon."

"Yes. After you didn't return, we left scouts on the other sides of the New Bristol gates. The one at Gate 2 picked up the beacon, which was curious enough. The pilot went to investigate, and that initiated a full recovery. One of our vessels picked you up, and then jumped back here to Ganymede. Well, to somewhere else first, but you were then brought here.

"It was really touch-and-go here for a while. No one was sure you were going to make it."

"Uh . . . was I hurt that bad?"

"Petty Officer Dalisay, you endured more Gs than anyone else has and lived, but 'lived' was a technicality. You were barely alive. Half of your organs were ruptured, and you had no brain activity. If your body hadn't been kept so cold, there would have been no recovery. For you or Doctor Moran."

No kidding? Lowering the temperature worked?

Then the fact that Dr. Tuominen said she had burst organs sunk in.

"Burst organs? I don't feel that bad," she said, lifting the sheet and looking at her belly.

"They've all been replaced, Petty Officer Dalisay," Dr. Tuominen said with a laugh. "Your new kidney's just started functioning yesterday, so the docs decided to slowly bring you around."

"New organs? Ma'am, how long was I out?"

"Four months. You've been here four months."

Beth stared at her in shock. *Four months! What about the Stingers? What about the war?* She shook her head in confusion.

"Ma'am, what's going on with the Stingers?"

"Your squadron? They're deployed now, so they're out of contact if you were planning on reaching out."

"Deployed again?"

We have five captured worlds. Yes, they are part of a major offensive. I can't really tell you more than that. But, I do have something for you," she said, taking out a chip and handing it to her.

"You won't be able to message back for the duration, but I need to remind you that everything you did, everything you told me, is classified. You won't discuss this with anyone, no matter how close you are with them. Understand?"

"Yes, ma'am."

"You did a great job, Petty Officer. If you ever feel like you're at a dead end, I can offer you quite a bit more in 5D. Just give me the word," she said before her eyes lost focus as people did when receiving messages.

She gave a small snort and said, "The hospital CO is outside the door here, demanding access with a horde of doctors. Seems they think they have dibs on your body for science, and they don't like me, a mere civilian, monopolizing your time."

"Oh, please save me," Beth said, only half-facetiously.

"Heavy lies the crown, or is it duty that's heavy," Dr. Tuominen said with a laugh. "But I'm afraid I'm powerless when doctors are on the rampage."

Beth looked at the chip in her hand. If she was going to be poked and prodded, she wouldn't have a chance to see the message for quite some time, unless she was mistaken.

"Can you at least delay them? I'd like to see my message first."

Dr. Tuominen smiled, then said, "I guess I can manage that."

The GT reached over to the hospital-issue tablet on the table beside the bed and handed it to her.

"This isn't a secure tablet," Beth said.

"Don't worry. There's nothing classified on that," Dr. Tuominen said. "And yes, we checked. Take care, Floribeth Salinas O'Shea Dalisay. Just give a shout when you're done."

She turned and walked to the door. A woman in a white lab coat started to enter, but the tall GT pushed her back, loudly announcing, "Petty Officer Dalisay will be with you in five minutes. Mr. Gerrity here will let you know when."

Beth smiled, then slid in the chip. Mercy, Fatboy, Hodar, Turtle, and Josh were crowded in a berthing space aboard a ship somewhere.

"Hey, sista mine!" Mercy said. "You done goofing off? What do they have you doing? Making the tours and showing off your medals for the war effort?"

"Fire Ant!" Fatboy boomed, sticking his head into the pick-up before Mercy shoved him back.

"They said we can send you a message before we take off. Can't tell you where we're going or what we're gonna be doing, 'cause, you know, op-security and all."

"Bullshit! It's because we don't know ourselves. We're mushrooms, you know, kept in the dark and fed shit!" Fatboy said, leaning in again.

"Satans' nuts, Fatboy. Quit hogging the cam," Mercy said, giving him a hard shot to the arm.

"You're the one hogging the cam," Fatboy said, rubbing where Mercy had punched him.

"That's 'cause Beth's my sister-in-law and bestie, so I get to hog it.

"Anyway," she said, looking back into the pick-up. "We heard you got yourself banged up, but you're fine. I don't know if you're gonna be joining us while we're deployed, but we're keeping a space warm for you. You even got a new Wasp. Sweet ride, this one."

"Yeah, your plane captain here about had an attack when he saw your old one," Hodar said.

"I did not!" Josh shouted.

"The hell he didn't. Cried like a baby," Mercy said. "Cried even more when the CO said they were going to deadline it."

"Well, I could have fixed it!" Josh insisted. "No need for a new one."

"Then why do you drool over the new one like a dog in heat?" Hodar asked.

"Eat me," Josh said, turning red.

"You sure you'd like that? I'm not a Wasp," Hodar said to the laughter of the others.

"Anyway, sista, we need to get down to legal for wills and that crap. I know, you'd think the ones we filled out five months ago would still be valid, but you know the Navy."

"All of you, tell Beth goodbye."

"Goodbye," everyone yelled out, not even close to being in unison. Fatboy didn't even say goodbye but "adios."

Mercy reached forward to cut the connection, then quickly shouted, "Your cousin Mary Anne had a baby. Rock's gonna be the godfather. Love ya, sista!"

The recording cut off. Beth leaned back, head on her pillow, a huge smile on her face. The message had done her a world of good. Even taking into account the fact that she'd been in an induced coma for the last four months, she'd still been away from her people for too long.

And that's what they were: her people. She missed them and wished she was out there in the deep black somewhere, getting ready to take on the crystals. She'd have to ask the impatiently waiting docs out there when she'd be able to join them. If she was going to miss this operation, then she'd catch the next one for sure. If she could escape a FAL-held world with a baby crystal, she sure the hell could escape a Navy hospital.

She hoped.

Dr. Tuominen's offer to join 5D was intriguing. If she took her up on that, she'd never be bored. Who knows how many worlds she'd surreptitiously visit?

Just like she'd done on New Bristol. But while she was proud of accomplishing the mission, she hadn't enjoyed it. It hadn't felt right.

Being in the Navy wasn't always enjoyable. Many of the times, hell, maybe most of them, it was pretty miserable. But it felt right. She was with her people, her tribe, and that alone would have made all the BS worth it.

But then there was the thrill she got when flying the *Tala*, when it was her against the enemy with everything at stake. It might not be PC, it might not be civilized, but she never felt as alive as when she was fighting the *Tala*, and she needed that adrenaline rush.

Dr. Tuominen's invitation was tempting, but right now, there was nowhere else Beth wanted to be than with the Stingers as they flew to fight the crystals.

Beth ejected the chip and slipped it in the small pocket over her heart. She took a deep breath, then yelled out, "OK, let them in."

Thank you for reading *Fortitude*. I hope you enjoyed this book, and I welcome a review on Amazon, Goodreads, or any other outlet.

If you would like updates on new books releases, news, or special offers, please consider signing up for my mailing list. Your email will not be sold, rented, or in any other way disseminated. If you are interested, please sign up at the link below:

http://eepurl.com/bnFSHH

OTHER BOOKS BY JONATHAN BRAZEE

The Navy of Humankind: Wasp Squadron
Fire Ant
Crystals
Ace

The United Federation Marine Corps
Recruit
Sergeant
Lieutenant
Captain
Major
Lieutenant Colonel
Colonel
Commandant

Rebel
(Set in the UFMC universe.)

Behind Enemy Lines
(A UFMC Prequel)

The Accidental War (A Ryck Lysander Short Story Published in *BOB's Bar: Tales from the Multiverse*)

The United Federation Marine Corps'
Lysander Twins
Legacy Marines
Esther's Story: Recon Marine

Noah's Story: Marine Tanker
Esther's Story: Special Duty
Blood United

Coda

Women of the United Federation Marine Corps
Gladiator
Sniper
Corpsman

High Value Target (A Gracie Medicine Crow Short Story)
BOLO Mission (A Gracie Medicine Crow Short Story)
Weaponized Math (A Gracie Medicine Crow Novelette,
Published in *The Expanding Universe 3. Nebula Award Finalist*)

The United Federation Marine Corps' Grub Wars
Alliance
The Price of Honor
Division of Power

Ghost Marines
Integration
Unification
Fusion

The Return of the Marines Trilogy
The Few
The Proud
The Marines

The Al Anbar Chronicles: First Marine Expeditionary Force--Iraq
Prisoner of Fallujah
Combat Corpsman
Sniper

Werewolf of Marines

Werewolf of Marines: Semper Lycanus
Werewolf of Marines: Patria Lycanus
Werewolf of Marines: Pax Lycanus

Soldier

Animal Soldier: Hannibal

To the Shores of Tripoli

Wererat

Darwin's Quest: The Search for the Ultimate Survivor

Venus: A Paleolithic Short Story

Secession

Duty

Semper Fidelis

Checkmate (Originally Published in The Expanding Universe 4)

Non-Fiction

Exercise for a Longer Life

The Effects of Environmental Activism on the Yellowfin Tuna Industry

Author Website

http://www.jonathanbrazee.com

Twitter

https://twitter.com/jonathanbrazee